THE CAPRICORN DECEPTION

MITCH HERRON 4

STEVE P. VINCENT

For Kirstie Close.

A true friend and warrior woman.

1

——————

"WHY NOW?" Mitch Herron's lips curled into a snarl, the sight so disgusting it turned his stomach, even after all the years he'd spent cleaning the sewers of humanity.

Clenching his fists, he changed his route through the Suva Municipal Market, the largest in Fiji's capital, to tail the Western tourist. The man was walking hand-in-hand with a Fijian girl who looked barely old enough to be in high school. He was wearing shorts and a white shirt that'd gone translucent with sweat, while the girl's clothes were inappropriate for her age, too small and too tight, her high heels causing her to walk as awkwardly as a baby giraffe.

Although he had somewhere to be, and this man wasn't the target of his operation, there was enough time for Herron to complete a little side job.

As they reached the edge of the market, it spilled out onto the road and coalesced with the rest of the capital. Herron stayed on their tail, maintaining his distance – patient and calculating – as the predator led his young prey to a less populated part of town. It wasn't hard, the girl walking slowly in the heels and the man oblivious to his surroundings, but when he saw the man reach down to squeeze the girl's ass Herron decided he'd seen enough.

He closed the distance and gave the man a brutal shot to the kidney. As he cried out in pain and staggered forward, Herron grabbed the girl around the waist and pulled her away.

"It's going to be all right," he said, crouching down to the girl's level. "I'll take you home soon."

She looked at Herron with wide eyes, then glanced at the man who'd been prepared to abuse her. "Okay."

Herron stood back to his full height, towering over the westerner, who was doubled over and struggling to breathe. Herron grabbed him by the collar of his shirt and dragged him, coughing and wheezing, down an alleyway that ran off the main street.

"Please, don't hurt me!" The man's voice was high-pitched with panic. "I can give you money!"

Herron clenched his jaw – he was going to teach this filth a lesson he'd never forget. He threw him to the ground and delivered several kicks into his torso, earning a grunt with each. Only when the man was whimpering and begging him to stop did Herron cease the punishment.

Herron growled. "You were going harm that little girl."

"No! I—"

Herron kicked him again. "Don't lie to me."

"I... I..."

Herron raised an eyebrow, waiting for a response. Instead, the man made a terrible mistake. Reaching into his pocket, he produced a small knife. He sat up on his haunches and held the blade out in front of him in a pitiful attempt to scare Herron off.

"I'd suggest you put that away," Herron said, keeping an eye on the knife. "Or this will get worse."

Instead, the fool ignored him and tried to climb to his feet, the knife still held in front of him.

Taking a step forward, Herron kicked him firmly in the chest, sending him sprawling and the knife flying from his grip.

Herron repeated his question. "The girl?"

"Yes!" The westerner's voice was pathetic. "I paid to be with her!"

"Have you done the same with others in the past?"

"Yes!"

Herron stepped closer and dug through the pedophile's pockets, meeting no resistance. He found an American passport in one pocket and a cellphone in the other. He now had the man's name and the only means for him to get out of the country.

He placed the cell on the ground in front of the animal.

"Call the police and give yourself up." Herron's voice was grave. "I'll be watching."

He thought the man might resist. Instead, he nodded, seemingly resigned to trying his luck with the Fijian Police Department over this wild man with fury in his eyes.

Herron waited while the man called the cops, admitted he was a child molester and told them where he was. When the call was done, Herron moved to the end of the alley and gestured for the girl to join him.

They waited in silence, Herron's eyes locked on the tourist, who was looking around as if desperate for a way out of all this. Eventually, a police car showed up and two officers arrested the man, taking his confession at face value. As they hauled him to the car and forced him into it, their faces were dark with the disdain reserved for child molesters.

When her would-be abuser had been hauled away, Herron turned to face the girl. "What's your name?"

She gave shy smile. "Lynda."

"Okay, Lynda, you're safe now." He tried his best to sound reassuring. "Where's your home?"

"A few minutes away."

Herron looked down at his watch. He had enough time to see her safely there, so he gestured for her to lead the way.

They wound their way through the streets of the capital and into the working-class heart of town, until they reached a modest house. Lynda looked back at Herron and ran inside when he nodded. He watched her enter the house, then turned and walked away.

His mind back on the job, he headed back toward the market. He hadn't made it far when, behind him, someone called out for him to stop. He ignored the shouts at first, not wanting to waste any more precious time, but they just became more insistent.

He turned around and saw a Fijian man waving. Herron sighed. "Can I help you?"

The local held his hand out. "I wanted to thank you for saving my daughter."

Herron shook his hand. "The man who was about to hurt her won't be able to hurt anyone again."

"Thank you, I—"

Herron smiled and interrupted. "Look, buddy, I really need to go. See you around."

The girl's father called after him. "My name is Jone Nath. You've a new friend for life!"

Herron resumed his walk back to the market, checking his watch again to confirm he had enough time for his mission. His target would be at the location – manning his market stall – until closing; about another half-hour. Then he'd leave to lead a protest march against Fiji's government.

The target's followers lovingly called him the General, on account of his ability to rouse a usually happy and contented populace into action. Herron had seen him at work a few times, standing in the crowd of a speech or a protest, the brash old man spewing vitriol about the corruption and incompetence of the current government. He might make an okay leader, but that wasn't for Herron to decide.

His masters had targeted the General for elimination.

It took five minutes to reach the market, crowded with people browsing all manner of food and goods. He snaked his way through the shoppers, searching for the General's stall, but when he arrived, the place was closed, its wares packed away and its owner nowhere to be seen.

The General, a man who was punctual to a fault, had left early.

Herron was looking around the market, searching for answers, when his phone rang. He dug it out of his pocket and answered. "Hello."

"You failed to eliminate the target." The electronically distorted voice chastised Herron. "The Fijian Army is leaving its barracks. The revolution has started and the General is leading it."

Herron's mouth fell open a little, then he steeled himself. "I was delayed. I only missed the target by a few minutes. There's still time."

"No." The voice of his handler was firm. "The army has mobilized and the people are on the streets. Intervening now would only cause more chaos. It's too late."

There was an explosion in the distance. Herron sighed. "I—"

His handler didn't let him finish. "Our client is displeased. Bug out and contact me when you're clear of the mission zone. A repeat performance of this failure will see your contract terminated."

Herron woke with a start, his eyes shooting open. He looked around, confused, until his mind recalibrated. He'd been dreaming. He rubbed his face. "Damn it."

He hadn't dreamed about his old life for over a year, not since he'd killed the Master and eradicated his corrupt former employers, the Enclave. He'd hoped the dreams were behind him, but it wasn't surprising they were back again. He was about to return to the location of the first mission he'd ever failed. And, despite learning later of the Enclave's self-serving agenda, it was one of his great regrets. His failure had led Fiji into to a decade of tyranny at the hands of the General, a man who'd gained the love of his people and overthrown a corrupt government, only to become something far worse.

Herron shouldn't be returning here at all. Since killing the Master and destroying his organization,

Herron had kept a low profile. From London, he'd taken the Channel Tunnel to Paris, where he'd accessed one of his cash stashes, then travelled to the southern tip of Italy. He'd bought a second-hand yacht in Sicily and then set sail for the South Pacific.

He'd found peace in paradise.

He lived as an ocean nomad, moving from island to island, never staying long enough for anyone to get used to him or ask too many questions. He never returned to the same place twice and never struck up any friendships. For most people, it'd be like a prison sentence, but Herron was used to being alone.

He liked it.

He closed his eyes and snoozed. As he drifted off, his mental shield was lowered once again and the shadows returned from their slumber to plague his. But again the evil was forced to retreat as he was woken by the gentle rocking of the yacht and the less subtle screech of ocean birds.

Resigned to starting the day, he dressed and headed for the main deck. Although the sun was shining, the day's heat hadn't yet arrived and there was a light breeze to help keep things cool. Herron took a few seconds to grip the siderail and enjoy the serenity. The sky and the Pacific Ocean were both a vivid blue, in contrast to the island in the distance.

"Time to get moving." He pushed himself off the rail. "Fiji, here I come."

In the wheelhouse, he pressed the button to pull up anchor and then got underway. When the boat was on course, he crouched down and pulled open a panel that housed lifejackets. He reached inside and felt around the back, being careful because the good start to the day could easily be undone if he wasn't.

He found the keypad at the back of the compartment and entered the code. At the same time as it clicked open a secret panel, the code also disarmed the bomb rigged to it. Herron had purchased the yacht cheap from an Italian mafia contact and now he used its several well-hidden smuggling compartments to hide his cash and valuables.

He pulled out a metal box and opened it. Inside were his insurance policies, taken from his Paris stash – tightly rolled wads of American dollars, a dozen fake passports and a silenced pistol. He pocketed a single roll of cash and chose one of the passports, then put the box back. Unfortunately, it was lighter than he'd like it to be, the money within having almost run out. That was why he was returning to Fiji, where he'd find the only stash he had in all of Asia. Those funds would keep him going for several more years, his boat fueled and his stomach full. The alternatives had been a return to Europe or the United States, and neither was a desirable option.

He stood and took the wheel again. As the minutes ticked by, the island grew before him, changing from a brown and green mass to an explosion of all types of color. Closer still, he could see signs of human development, the buildings of the capital and seaside berths for ships and smaller vessels. The whole time, he kept the yacht travelling straight and slow, not wanting to draw any more attention to his arrival than necessary.

When he was a nautical mile from the Royal Suva Yacht Club, he was hailed over the radio. "This is the

Fijian Immigration Department, please identify yourself."

Herron lifted the radio. "My name is Robert Sochi, skippering the *Erica* on an American passport. Do you require any more information?"

"Please hold."

Herron waited a few minutes, one hand on the wheel and one hand on the radio, until finally the permission came in. His fake identification was good enough to pass a casual inspection, so he didn't expect any trouble from the authorities, but he hadn't survived a year on the run by being careless. He'd land here just long enough to make his way into the capital and secure his stash, then he'd return to the boat and depart as quickly as possible.

He was told to berth in the Yacht Club and show his documents, but that no visa was required. He'd expected that, given his fake passport was from the United States, a visa-exempt country. And, just like that, he'd be past the only official check of his arrival in Fiji.

He was back in paradise, but he hoped to be gone again just as easily.

* * *

It hadn't taken long for him to realize something felt wrong about the island.

After passing through immigration, Herron had left the Royal Suva Yacht Club and headed south in the direction of the Suva Municipal Market. The walk had taken about twenty minutes. Following the path along the coastline, he'd immediately noticed there was a lack of tourists, their numbers far fewer than he remembered.

A decade ago, Fiji had been bustling with them, and the locals had taken to them warmly. Now, dressed in khaki shorts and a pale green shirt, and looking the picture of a casual American visitor, he was attracting glances – resentful, suspicious and unwelcoming.

He kept his hands in his pockets as he strolled through the market. A mass of locals and the occasional tourist fought for space amongst the stalls, and he was soon in the middle of the scrum as he browsed the wares.

The glares continued, eyes locked onto him wherever he walked. Nothing was too overt and nobody challenged him directly, but there were enough sideways glances and pursed lips to make it clear something was off. It made him even more determined to get his stash and then get the hell out of Fiji, but first he had one other thing to do.

Reaching the center of the market, where the General's stall had been so many years ago, he felt a pang of regret.

The stall was about twenty square feet, with waist-high walls dividing it from its neighbors. There was still a counter at the front, still a corroded metal sign screwed to it, advertising the stall's goods and prices. That's where the similarities ended.

The sign had been graffitied with a range of vulgar suggestions about the General, and the stall had been splattered with red paint, the top of the counter covered in red handprints. It was a pretty obvious sign at least a portion of the populace was unhappy with the General.

Herron lingered outside for another minute, contemplating his failure and what it had done to the people on this island. He'd killed a lot of innocent people on behalf of the Enclave, a sin he'd atoned for by eradicating the organization, but in this case the kill would've been justified.

With a sigh, Herron continued on his way. He found his way to the public bathroom in the market, checked that the place was empty, then locked himself in one of the stalls. He put the toilet lid down, sat atop it and waited for almost a minute. When it was clear nobody else had followed him, he looked up.

And smiled.

In a changing world, it was impossible to guarantee his stashes would remain in place. Some were in bank vaults, others were in railway-station lockers, while others still were in wall cavities or similar hiding places. Here, in Fiji, he'd been pressed for time and options, so he'd decided to put the money right where he'd failed his mission.

He got to his feet, stood on the toilet lid and then reached up for the ceiling. It was easy enough to lift and move one of the tiles aside. He reached up inside, his heart pounding in fear that his stash might've been discovered, but eventually he found the box wrapped in a plastic bag.

Breathing a sigh of relief, he took it and climbed down, not bothering to replace the tile. He removed the box from the bag and opened it, revealing several wads of cash, more IDs and another pistol. He stuffed all the money into his pockets, but he left the other items behind. He had enough guns and identification aboard the yacht and there was no telling when he might need to hit this hiding place again.

After replacing the box and the tile, he washed his hands and left.

He bought a bottle of soda before heading back through the market to the exit. There was still tension in the air, but he was unable to identify a specific threat. He didn't know what dangers lurked nearby, or what political fires were smoldering on the island, but he didn't want to find out, either. Anonymity was his friend and he wanted no part of whatever was wrong on here.

The island didn't care.

As he walked the path back to the Yacht Club, he slowed to a stop and his eyes widened. The foreign visitors who populated the Yacht Club were spewing onto the streets, running in all directions and screaming. Pursuing them up the road was a group of Fijian men with blades and blunt weapons, attacking those they could catch.

Tourists ran past him, terrified and bloody, their attackers close behind. There was no way he could stay out of this, given the thugs and their victims were between him and his yacht. He sighed. "Fuck."

He charged straight at the closest Fijian, who swung at him with a blood-streaked machete. Herron deflected the blow with his soda bottle, the glass somehow remaining intact until he smashed it over the Fijian's head. He stabbed the broken neck into the man's throat, and as the surprised Fijian reached up to the blood suddenly pouring from his throat, Herron seized his wrist and bent it back. The machete dropped to the sand and Herron head-butted its former owner, dropping him. Maybe he'd survive if someone called in medical care in time, but Herron didn't care.

The important thing for him was he was armed.

After reaching down to pick up the machete, he waited for the next attacker to come at him, a younger Fijian wielding a switchblade. The man inched closer, hesitant, so Herron changed his plan. He stepped forward and hacked the machete at his chest, slashing deep enough release a spray of blood that painted the sidewalk crimson.

The knifeman howled and fled.

Two down, but there were plenty still rampaging through the Yacht Club. Three of them now surrounded Herron, preventing him from pressing his attack. Using the machete on any one of them would expose his back to the others.

Herron turned on the spot, watching for anyone making a move, playing for time. He glanced at each of his foes in turn, sensing their wariness given he'd just put down two of their friends. "Who's next?"

The biggest and meanest looking of the three hefted a steel bar in his hand and spat at Herron. "You made a big mistake. We're going to fuck you up."

Herron smirked. "You and what army?"

The Fijian gave a knowing smile. "The Movement."

"The Movement?" Herron laughed. "Like feminism or civil rights?"

The Fijian glowered. "There's a revolution coming and parasites like you must help to pay for it."

The trio approached him all at once, like water bursting from a dam.

He stepped forward and slashed at the Fijian holding a steel bar. The man flinched away, too slow, a cut opening on his cheek.

Herron pressed the attack, the Fijian deflecting his strikes.

Then the others were on him.

A heavy blow cracked the back of his head and stars exploded before Herron's eyes. He grunted, dropped to one knee, his vision blurry. He tried to get back to his feet, but a second impact to his head knocked him off balance and sent him to the ground. After landing hard, Herron huddled into a ball, protecting his head as they kicked into him.

Whistles and shouting penetrated the sound of the blows raining down on him. Immediately, the abuse ceased and the attackers fled.

Herron climbed to his hands and knees and shook his head to clear it. He looked towards the Yacht Club and saw the attackers were long gone.

"Sir!" Someone nearby shouted. "He's moving!"

A uniformed Fijian cop was walking over to him. The officer was young – about twenty years old – and eyed Herron with a deep suspicion, his gun held down by his side. A second, more senior cop, also with his gun drawn, approached behind him.

"What's your name?" The senior officer asked. His uniform was well-worn and sported the most stripes of rank. "Are you badly hurt?"

"Bob Sochi." Herron lied, rattling off the name on his fake passport. "And no, I'm fine. Just shaken up. Actually, my yacht is berthed here and I need to get back to it."

"You need to do what you're told." The cop's voice was heavy with threat. "We have some questions for you."

Herron got to his feet. Conversations with the authorities wouldn't help him stay anonymous, but being recalcitrant was an even worse idea. If he answered their questions right here, he could be on his way within a few minutes. If he refused, he could spend the night in a cell.

"What do you want to know?"

"I want to know why you ran toward the attackers while everybody else ran away." The cop raised an eyebrow. "I want to know how you are skilled enough to take down two armed men, wound another, and slow all of them down long enough to allow dozens of people to flee to safety. I want to know who you are."

"I didn't think about it," Herron said. "I have some military experience and my training took over. Can I go now?"

"I'm afraid not." The cop shrugged. "The General has closed all ports of departure and the Yacht Club is in lockdown. This was one of a dozen coordinated attacks across the capital and we need to get to the bottom of it. Once we do, you'll be allowed to leave."

"But I—"

"This isn't a discussion, Mr Sochi." The cop cut him off. "I recommend you go to the hospital and get checked out. If not, you're welcome to book a hotel and enjoy the sights for a day or two. But you're not getting to your boat."

Herron sighed, but then he nodded. There was no arguing with the cops. He watched as the two officers walked away, more of their colleagues swarming the scene, stopping anyone from entering. Like it or not, it looked like he was stuck here, forced to spend days when he'd only wanted to spend hours.

Could his timing have been any worse?

Coordinated attacks, they'd said, and the Fijian had mentioned something called The Movement. Herron didn't know why this Movement had decided to challenge the General now, but he knew what they wanted. From barren deserts to lush jungles to tropical paradises to sprawling metropolises, the currency of mankind was the same the world over: some people had power and would do anything to protect it, while others wanted it and would do the unthinkable to get it.

He'd had seen power struggles just like this a hundred times all over the world.

He'd been *involved* a lot of them.

But not this time.

"Assholes," he muttered, and walked away from the Yacht Club.

So much for stealth.

2
_____

HERRON PLACED a jerry can full of gasoline, a six-pack of Coke, a packet of cleaning cloths and a funnel onto the counter. He smiled at the gas station cashier. "I'll take all this, a pack of Marlboros and a lighter."

"You're an American?" The attendant frowned at Herron. "I'm surprised you haven't been caught up in all the trouble."

Herron shrugged. He tossed some banknotes on the counter in front of the cashier. "Does that cover it?"

The cashier's frown turned into a grin when he saw the American dollars. He scooped up the notes, placed some change on the counter – in Fijian dollars – and procured the cigarettes and the lighter from a shelf behind him. As he bagged it all up, Herron pocketed the change, then took his purchases and left.

He'd stuck around for a full day after the attack. The cracks on his head and kicks to the body hadn't needed medical attention beyond what he could do with the hotel first aid kit, so he'd just waited, hoping the General would open up the ports. Things hadn't quite gone to plan, though. Several more attacks had put the capital on edge and the streets were filled with soldiers and cops, particularly anywhere frequented by Westerners.

With the Yacht Club on lockdown, if he wanted to get off the island, he'd need to clear the way first. The bag from the gas station would help with that.

He walked up the coast until he was only thirty yards from the Yacht Club entrance, then started scanning each house that fronted it. They were nice homes and it looked like most of them had been built in the last few years, since natural gas had been found on the island. Everywhere Herron looked, it seemed money was pouring into Fiji, which made the turmoil surprising. Nothing drove money away faster than political turmoil.

With a shrug, he settled on a house that'd suit his task. He rang the bell and waited, until eventually he heard movement from the other side of the door. A deadbolt unlocked with a heavy clunk, the door opened an inch and an eye appeared in the crack, staring at him suspiciously.

"Hi!" Herron gave his best disarming smile. "I was wondering if you could help me out for a moment."

"With what?" The woman on the other side of the door sounded cautious, which wasn't surprising given the situation on the streets.

"I need access to your roof." Herron slowly dug into his pocket and pulled out some cash. "I can pay you very well."

"I'm not interested in your money. I don't want any part of all this trouble." She started to close the door. "Goodb—"

Herron put his foot in the door, keeping it open. "I think you should reconsider."

"Who're you?" The homeowner's eyes widened in fear. "I'll call the police..."

"The police won't help you. Take the money."

He held out a good chunk of his remaining cash and she looked at the money for the first time. At last, she relented, stepping back into the hallway and letting him inside. Herron handed her the bills.

He fixed her with a hard glare. "Roof?"

The woman pointed to the back of the house.

Finding a staircase, he climbed to the top and through a small door that accessed the outside. From there, he looked out over the Yacht Club and took in the situation. His yacht was berthed the furthest from the road and there were far too many cops for him to reach it. He needed to get them to focus on something else – like a fresh attack from the terrorists on the Westerners.

He pulled the Coke bottles from the bag and emptied them. Next, he put the funnel in one of the bottles, unscrewed the cap of the jerry can and poured in some gasoline. He repeated the process five times and then set the jerry can aside. Lastly, he tore the cleaning cloths into strips and fed one into each of the bottle necks.

He now had six of Molotov's finest cocktails to get the attention of Fiji's police.

Dusk was settling in, the sunset casting the ocean in a brilliant burnt-orange color. Herron picked up a bottle, took the lighter and lit the strip of cloth. Then he hefted the Molotov as far as he could in the direction of the Yacht Club's main building.

He smiled as it sailed through the air, the flaming

cloth acting like a tracer, then smashed against the roof. Flames immediately spread across the top of the building, as the gasoline inside the bottle sprayed over a wide area and caught fire. He repeated the process with the other bottles. Four hit the roof and one went through a window.

The result was spectacular.

Herron knew the effect on the outside of the building would be to cause drama rather than any real damage. Inside, it was a different story. Soon, flames were burning with uncontrolled fury, smoke spewing from the windows. Cops swarmed to the burning building from all around the Yacht Club.

It was exactly what Herron had wanted.

He left the rooftop, ran down the stairs, back through the woman's home and out the front door, joining other Fijians who'd emerged from their homes and were streaming toward the burning building to help.

Except, instead of helping to put out the fire and rescue anyone inside, he dived into the water.

As the darkness of night descended on the island, Herron paddled through the water under the boardwalk, using it to cover his approach to the *Erica*. He moved as silent as a sea snake, until he reached the hull. Only then was he forced to emerge from cover, climb up onto the boardwalk and sneak onto the boat.

As he moved to the living hatch below deck, he saw the lock had been smashed. He slid the door open and entered the cabin, a small living area and galley combination. Nothing looked out of place, until he saw an envelope on the table. He picked it up and tore it open. Inside was a piece of paper with a message.

I know who you are.
I know you tried to kill me all those years ago.
I have a job for you.
If you refuse, I expose you to the Americans.
If you comply, you're free to go.
I am at Government House.

Herron stared at the note, fury building within him, then screwed it into a ball and hurled it away.

The General was trying to *blackmail* him?

He changed into dry shorts and another casual shirt, then made his way to the wheelhouse, where he repeated the process to disarm the bomb and unlock the panel behind the lifejackets. The fact that the bomb hadn't gone off told him his stash would be untouched, and he pulled out the box and opened it. He put most of the cash back inside, exchanging it for the pistol, then replaced everything, reset the bomb and returned to the deck.

He gripped the siderail of his boat with one hand and his pistol with the other, looking back towards Suva.

The most dangerous predator on the island had a new target in his sights.

Constantly searching for handholds and using his feet push him higher, Herron scaled the ten-meter-high stone wall. Halfway up, he looked left and right, making sure no soldiers had lucked upon him. Although he was moving quietly, trying to sneak into Government House – the headquarters of the Fijian dictator – was dicey.

But he had a date with the General.

He was glad that things in the Pacific were a little more relaxed than in America. Back home, any equivalent facility would have cameras and sensors, razor wire and armed sentries. Here, it was just a high wall and some threatening signs. The government seemed content to show its power in other ways, like the hundreds of troops on the streets.

It made breaking in a little easier.

Satisfied he hadn't been spotted, Herron reached the top of the wall and perched on it. He could see a couple of sentries on the gate and a few more on patrol inside the grounds. The buildings at the center of the compound were well lit, but the lawn skirting the inside perimeter was shrouded in darkness.

Perfect.

Herron jumped off the wall and landed on the grass, crouching to soften the landing. Standing upright, he drew his pistol. He was far less prepared than he'd liked to be, and had no idea where the General was, so he figured he'd start with the nicest building.

Moving across the lawn like a shadow, he approached the main structure. It looked like it had been constructed recently, at odds with the rest of the colonial-era buildings.

Herron focused his attention on a side window. One other advantage of undertaking a mission in Fiji was the heat. While secure military buildings in other places might be buttoned up tight, this one had several windows open to catch the cooler evening breeze. He stuck his head inside, looked around, and confirmed the coast was clear before climbing in.

He moved through a dark, empty cubicle farm, the

men and women who worked there gone home for the night. Keeping low, he stopped near the doorway.

Footsteps.

Herron peeked into the hallway and saw a woman in civilian clothes walking away from him. He slipped out of the room and followed her, ready to pounce if she became aware of his presence. Instead, she slipped into another room. He followed her inside, closed the distance to her and clamped his hand over her mouth.

"Mmmm!" She was panicking, tensing and inhaling sharply through flared nostrils. He pressed the barrel of the pistol hard against her back. "Stay calm and you'll live."

She gathered herself together and nodded vigorously.

Herron eased the pressure on the pistol just a little, to show that her cooperation would be rewarded. "I'm going to remove my hand from your mouth. Don't scream."

She nodded again.

Herron slowly lowered his grip to her neck, to keep her in control. "Where's the General?"

"His office is at the top of the stairs." Her voice was wavering with fear and her body was stiff. "Please, don't hurt me."

"I'm not here to hurt you. I'm here for the General."

Her body relaxed at his words. "Good."

Clearly, she was no fan of the dictator.

"I need to tie you up while I take care of business," he told her. "Someone will be along to free you soon, though."

After another nod, he gestured for her to sit in an office chair. He'd brought no restraints, so he improvised, pulling an extension cord from the wall and using it to bind her waist to the back of the chair. She'd be able to get out of it, but it should buy him enough time to take care of business with the General.

When he was finished with the makeshift bonds, Herron looked down at her. "Stay here, stay quiet and nobody else will be harmed."

He backtracked up the hall, found the stairs and went up them two at a time. Now on the second floor, he walked through the open door to the General's office, where he found the Fijian military leader standing at his window and staring out into the night.

Herron cleared his throat and smiled when the General flinched and turned, his eyes widening when he realized he wasn't alone. "You and I have some matters to discuss."

To his credit, the General regained his composure within a second, a neutral expression on his face as he sized up Herron. "How many of my men are dead?"

"None." Herron kicked the door closed with his heel then stepped closer to the General. "You're playing a dangerous game with me."

The General didn't respond right away. He was an old man, with greying hair and carrying a little too much weight, but he exuded confidence. "I'm used to playing dangerous games, Mr *Sochi*. I started about a decade ago, when I led a movement that overthrew a monster. A movement that was almost stillborn because of you."

Herron said nothing.

"Oh yes, I know all about your little mission to kill me all the way back then. I ran the market then, just like I do now. A hundred pairs of eyes noticed you then, just as they did now. This is a small community. I see everything and, while I don't know your real name, I know you're on the Interpol and FBI watch lists."

Herron fumed silently. A year of successfully hiding in plain sight and all his efforts to stay out of the deadly game would be wasted because of this old man.

"Now where once I overthrew, others are seeking to overthrow *me*," the General said. "They accuse me of things I haven't done, align themselves with criminals and anarchists. They commit terrorist attacks on my government and my people. So, Mr Sochi, you're about to join *my* dangerous game."

Fury rose in Herron's gut. He closed the distance between them, gripped the General by the throat and slammed him into the wall, driving the breath from the Fijian leader. He jammed his pistol up under the General's chin and all of the leader's mirth disappeared immediately. It did for most men who were the pull of a trigger away from death.

Herron let the gravity of the situation sink in, then he tried one more time. "I have no interest in you or your fight. You should let me leave and forget I was ever here."

The General shrugged. "Shoot me. Even if you evade my men and get back to your boat, you're finished. Your face will be all over the news within hours, the name of your boat on coastguard lists the world over. Nowhere will be safe for you. There's only one way we both get what we want."

Herron's eyes blazed with anger as the words sank in. Once, he'd have maimed and destroyed all he needed to persevere, but now he was alone in the world, with dwindling resources and nowhere to turn. He was vulnerable and isolated. He exhaled slowly, released the pressure on the General's throat just a little, but left the gun right where it was.

"That's better." The General coughed and drew in a deep breath. "I don't need much from you, just a little clean-up. If you take care of it for me, you can leave with my blessing."

Herron remained silent. Waiting.

"Despite our efforts to improve the economy and living standards, my administration has been plagued by indiscriminate violence and turmoil orchestrated by a small group of malcontents." The General shrugged. "When my forces respond, the rebels melt away to another part of the island, until they're ready to strike again."

"So you need some hired help?"

"Unfortunately, my military isn't vast. Securing the city under martial law, dealing with the Movement in Suva and making sure other parts of the island are protected from the rebels has stretched my resources. I only have reserve forces left available to me and they're not experienced enough to get this job done. If you help me, I won't expose you and you can leave Fiji."

Herron knew the General had him in check.

He nodded.

3

GRIPPING HIS RIFLE, Herron crept through the forest, careful to check where his foot would land before each step. The last thing he needed was to step on a branch, alerting his foes. His caution made for slow going, but he was in no hurry. While he didn't know where his targets were located, they didn't know he was coming either. He had all night if he needed it.

After Herron had agreed to his terms, the General had explained that his men had tracked the Movement to the forest near Suva. Each time he'd deployed scouts to find the rebel camp, however, his men had disappeared without a trace. Whether they were dead or simply prisoners was immaterial to the General. All that mattered was they'd failed.

Now the Fijian leader had hopes that one man could succeed where many troops hadn't. He'd ordered Herron to find the camp, kill the leader of the Movement and then radio in the location of the camp. That was the price of freedom – the assassination of a terrorist who'd targeted civilians indiscriminately in his campaign to overthrow the nation's leader. When the bill was paid, Herron could go.

He'd been given a choice of weaponry and had settled for a scoped sniper rifle, his own silenced pistol, a machete, a knife and a mix of grenades. He'd also borrowed jungle camo, combat webbing to carry his gear and night-vision goggles. It wasn't his usual operational loadout, but he had enough tools to get the job done.

He'd been searching for hours, pushing deeper into the forest, yet he'd found no sign of any camps. He was starting to wonder if the General's intelligence about the Movement's location was right. Fiji wasn't a large place, but there'd still be plenty of places for a determined resistance to hide – forests, mountains or even in their own homes.

He continued for another quarter-hour, rifle at the ready and his senses on a razor's edge. He'd been worried that his lack of action in recent months had dulled his edge, but now he was back in the field he felt primed.

If he hadn't been, he might've missed the glimmer of moonlight on metal.

"You bastards." Herron's voice was a whisper as he pulled his foot back and planted it where it had been before.

A steel wire had been stretched across the way ahead of him.

Herron sharpened his senses, searching for an ambush but seeing nothing except the trees and hearing nothing but the soft rustle of the breeze in their leaves. Satisfied he was still alone, he turned his attention to the device.

He inspected the wire first. It ran from a pile of leaves to the nearest tree and then from that tree across to the next one. Pegs with rings for the wire to run through had been driven into the trunks. A stumbling idiot – anyone other than Herron – would've tripped the wire and unleashed whatever nasty was beneath the leaves.

Herron crouched down and gently felt around the mound of dirt and leaves, being very careful to avoid the wire. When he couldn't feel anything obvious on the outskirts of the mound, he inspected more closely.

Then he inhaled sharply, as he realized what the trap contained.

Manufactured in America for use during the Vietnam War, M16 bounding anti-personnel mines were still in use decades later. He'd almost fallen victim to one himself in the jungles of Cambodia a few years ago, undertaking a mission on behalf of the Enclave. While he'd survived that encounter, he was still wary of the devices.

After being triggered, the M16 was designed to leap a few feet into the air, pushed up by an initial high-explosive charge. Once at waist-height, a second charge went off, spreading deadly steel shards in a 360-degree arc. It was a malicious and indiscriminate weapon to deploy in a forest where children or other civilians could trigger it, but the Movement had done just that.

Sure, The General was a tyrant, but this confirmed there was evil on both sides of the conflict in Fiji and now Herron was even more determined to end The Movement. He'd take his anger out on the rebel leader personally.

He pulled out his knife and used it to carefully

unearth the landmine. First, he scraped away the dirt and leaves, painstakingly revealing the trap. Once he'd cleared as much off the top as he could, he used the blade to dig a trench around the device, until it was sitting on its own in a shallow hole like a castle surrounded by a moat.

Moving with the precision of a surgeon and the concentration of a high-stakes gambler, Herron went to work. He inserted a pin into the wire-strung trigger, removing its ability to detonate. Next, he dug into his vest and pulled out a set of pliers. He positioned the taut tripwire in between the blades of the pliers, held his breath and cut.

Nothing happened.

Herron got to his feet. After placing the pliers back into his combat vest and his knife back in its sheath, he picked up the mine. Even though he had the pin in the trigger and nothing would set it off, he didn't want to leave the device in the middle of the forest. Instead, he tethered it to his combat vest.

With the insidious trap rendered inert, Herron lifted his rifle and moved on. Now he had even more motivation to destroy the Movement's leadership. He'd agreed to the General's request to secure passage from Fiji, but the chance to wipe out scum who'd lay mines was an added bonus.

He was going to enjoy this.

* * *

"Fiji..." Herron spoke in a soft, mocking voice as he removed his night-vision goggles and wiped his soaked brow with his hand. "It's a paradise..."

He put the goggles back in place and pressed on. Hours after finding the landmine, he still hadn't located the resistance camp and the flicker of hope he'd felt that he was close had been doused under inches of rain. He didn't want to return to the General empty-handed, but he didn't want to spend all night wandering the forest in a biblical storm, either.

The weather had turned nasty at three in the morning, battering the island. Thunder was booming, lightning was flashing and rain was hammering down relentlessly. His visibility was shot, he couldn't hear a thing and he was soaked through. It was the wildest storm Herron had ever seen and he was right in the middle of it.

He stalked from tree to tree as rain fell relentlessly. If he didn't find the Movement's camp by dawn, he'd need to bug out. He was well-equipped and well-trained, so he had all the advantages during the night, but as soon as daylight struck the odds would shift drastically against him.

Then, just as he was considering this, two men appeared.

The rain had cooled the forest to the point where Herron's night-vision goggles showed nothing else as a heat source, so the men were lit up like Las Vegas. They flared bright as the sun as they ambled through the forest toward him, no doubt soaked through and miserable. But they were both armed with rifles and had sided with an organization that had no problem recklessly planting landmines.

That made them fair game.

Herron pressed his back against a tree, close enough to be invisible in the current conditions. He placed the butt of his rifle on the ground, leaned the barrel against the tree and drew his knife. Hidden by the tree trunk, as still as a rock and as silent as the dead, he tracked the men until they passed him.

Then he exploded with violence.

Herron closed the distance to them in two powerful strides, grabbed the closest man's hair and yanked back on it. As the rebel let out a yelp of surprise, Herron dug the knife into his back. In seconds, he stabbed the man six times; on the seventh, the blade stuck.

He let go of the Fijian's hair and his victim dropped, the knife still buried inside him.

His first victim already forgotten, Herron shifted his focus to the second, who'd turned to face him. Before the man could get the weapon into a firing position, Herron grabbed its barrel then stepped closer and delivered a brutal headbutt. The guerilla cried out in pain and staggered back, releasing his grip on the rifle and allowing Herron to snatch it away.

Herron took aim. "If you tell me where your camp is, I'll let you walk out of here."

The injured man backed away, hand to his face, blood from his destroyed nose streaming between his fingers. "No!"

He turned and ran, sloshing through mud in the darkness. But Herron had the advantage of night-vision, so he gave chase and tackled him to the ground. They struggled for a moment, until Herron grabbed the back of the Fijian's skull in a vice-like grip and pushed his face into the mud.

Herron's muscles strained to hold the rebel's face under the mud as he thrashed and struggled to breathe. He must've been in excruciating pain, his broken nose pressing into the ground. Herron hoped it'd give him an incentive to part with the information, because the guy he'd stabbed wouldn't be talking any time soon.

After holding the man under for 10 seconds, Herron lifted his head out of the mud and whispered in his ear. "Tell me where your camp is!"

"Okay!" The Fijian sputtered, sucking in desperate, heaving breaths and spitting out the mud in his mouth. "I'll tell you!"

Herron released him, drew his pistol and pressed the barrel into the back of his skull. "Don't fuck it up."

The man shook his head and then gestured with his chin. "We're camped a mile in that direction. By a stream."

Herron considered for a moment, trying to figure out if the rebel was telling the truth. In his experience, men who thought they were at the end of their lives didn't lie so much. He eased the pressure of the pistol barrel against the man's head.

"Normally I'd kill you now." Herron reached into his combat vest for the zip ties he carried for this exact purpose. "Lucky for you, I'm just going to tie you up."

* * *

Having already scouted the perimeter for patrols and found nothing of note, Herron lay prone in the mud, with the Movement's camp about 700 yards ahead of him. It was a sorry sight: just a few dozen tents, with double that number of people getting battered by the weather, as they huddled under canvas awnings.

He suspected he was looking at the sum total of the Movement.

Keeping his eyes on the camp, Herron lifted the cap on one end of his rifle scope and then the other, exposing the high-quality optics to the elements for the first time. Although the gun was wet, he'd managed to keep it out of the mud and it'd fire just fine.

He looked down the sights and chambered a round, starting to search for his target. The rebels had enough lights and lanterns around the place he'd almost be better using his natural eyesight.

As he scanned their faces and searched for his target, he got a good understanding of the Movement. This was a ragtag group of partisans who relied on terror and surprise in their campaign against the government. It was hard to believe that such a motley crew could cause carnage all across Fiji, but then again, similar tactics had been used to good effect for centuries.

At last he saw the Movement's leader, his primary target, carrying a rifle and looking exactly like the man in the photo the General had shown him. A former soldier, the soon-to-be-dead man was huddled under a makeshift shelter with several other people, an uninspiring leader of a makeshift army.

Herron lined up the shot, the crosshairs from the rifle scope aligning perfectly with his target's head. Even in perfect conditions, 700 yards was no easy shot. In this weather, it was even harder, but he was confident he could make the shot.

As the thunder roared in the sky, Herron fired. The rifle kicked into his shoulder, the sound of the shot masked by the elements.

His aim was true, his target dead before he hit the ground.

The camp exploded with action. Some screamed, some ran away. Some picked up weapons, others threw them down, clearly thinking the Fijian Army had sharpshooters in the trees and that to resist would be to die. Amidst all the chaos, the authorities would have no trouble mopping up these men.

Herron prepared to bug out, then froze in shock.

A man sporting a tactical headset and carrying a submachine gun was emerging from one of the tents. The gun alone was out of place, a modern weapon amongst the relics carried by the resistance fighters, but the real concern was the headset.

It meant the man had someone to talk to.

It meant he had friends who could be brought to bear...

Suddenly, everything Herron thought he'd known about the Movement had changed.

The ragged resistance was backed up by something substantial, he was sure of that now.

He used his GPS locator to determine his current coordinates and then radioed the General. He spoke in only a whisper and said nothing except the longitude and latitude, just enough to bring down the hammer on the Movement and their mysterious ally.

Thirty minutes passed, the Movement sending patrols out into the night to look for the shooter. None of them came close to finding him. Meanwhile, the camp was being dismantled painfully slowly. The rebels had no vehicles, so whatever they took with them had to be carried on their backs.

They had no hope of catching Herron or of departing before the General's men arrived.

Whereas Herron had approached the camp as

silently as a spider, the Fijian Army unit sent to crush the Movement arrived as loud as an elephant. They approached from the south – the opposite direction Herron had come from – gunfire roaring in the forest as the resistance members who'd been packing up the camp gave up and joined the fight.

Less than two minutes after the engagement started, his suspicions were proven correct. Over the occasional boom of thunder, the chatter of gunfire and the constant sound of rainfall, he could hear the *thump-thump-thump* of choppers on approach. He put his night-vision goggles back on and could immediately see the heat signature of two choppers in the sky.

The rebel cavalry had arrived.

Herron focused on the men who were rappelling out of the chopper, right on top of the camp. He counted sixteen of them; not an overwhelming force, but if the mercenaries were any good, they might be able to tip the balance against the Fijian Army.

The General wasn't only fighting a resistance, he was also pitted against a well-organized and well-equipped band of soldiers for hire. It further confirmed that the island was a powder keg and Herron didn't want to be around when it exploded.

He climbed up out of the mud, hefted his rifle and withdrew.

Time to reclaim his freedom.

4

HERRON CLIMBED out of the Army jeep that'd carried him back to Suva and to the front gate of Government House – a more direct approach than his previous entry. The guards had clearly been expecting him, because once they'd taken away his weapons they'd escorted him straight to the General's office.

Herron approached the General's desk. "The leader of the Movement is dead. I took his head clean off."

The General steepled his fingers and looked up. "And then you called my men into an ambush. My forces were picked apart by the Movement and their mercenary allies, who then escaped."

Herron shrugged. "You told me to take out the leader and radio the location of the camp. I did both. You *didn't* tell me about their mysterious allies."

"That was on a need-to-know basis. The mercenaries are hired by a Chinese resource company intent on increasing its presence on Fiji. It—"

Herron held up a hand. "I did what you asked. Now you'll do as you promised."

The General sized Herron up as if he might refuse his request, then picked up his phone and made a call, rattling off a few words in Fijian before hanging up. "I've summoned a driver for you. He will take you to the Yacht Club and escort you aboard your vessel. Leave immediately and never return to Fiji. If you show up again or interfere in my business, that mistake will be fatal. Am I clear?"

Herron nodded. "Okay."

"It was a pleasure doing business with you, Mr Sochi." The General looked behind Herron as a door opened and a soldier stepped into the office. "Now get off my island."

Herron followed the soldier out, down the stairs to the ground level and through the front door. It was a relief to have his freedom back in sight, but still he kept alert. He wouldn't relax until he was back on the boat and far out to sea. The General was far too devious to trust.

When they reached the car, Herron climbed into the back seat and the driver set off in the direction of the Yacht Club. Through the window, he saw armored vehicles and troops on the streets, keeping the city in the General's iron grip. It was a smart move. Now the Movement had been decapitated, whatever was left would be easily crushed – a perfect case study in consolidating power.

Herron's eyes narrowed as the car's radio crackled, filling the vehicle with the grave, authoritative voice of a man speaking in Fijian. The driver's frown as he listened to the message was clearly visible in the rearview mirror. Whatever was happening, it was serious.

Herron waited for the chatter to stop and then leaned forward in his seat. "What the hell is going on?"

The driver snapped out of his serious mood, looking at Herron in the mirror and smiling. "Nothing that'll prevent you from getting away from the island."

His assurance didn't fill Herron with confidence.

Sensing Herron's skepticism, the driver continued. "The families of members of the Movement are being rounded up and sent to Suva Prison."

Herron knew the place: it had been under construction when he'd first been on the island, used to house the dissidents and annoyances the General wanted out of the way. He doubted anything good happened inside.

He sat back in his seat and retreated into his own mind. There was so much evil in Fiji he felt like he was drowning in it. But while good sense was telling him to stay out of it and get the hell off the island, his conscience nagged at him. The members of the Movement knew the risks and had chosen their fate, but their families shouldn't be made to suffer for those choices.

Could Herron really turn his back on them?

The driver kept his eyes on the road, oblivious to Herron's dilemma. Similar men were now ferrying innocent people to prison, and the thought made Herron's blood boil. When at last the vehicle pulled to a stop outside the Yacht Club, Herron sat, frozen by indecision. The driver turned in his seat, a look of confusion on his face.

Then Herron delivered a brutal right hook that knocked the man out cold.

He climbed out of the car, opened the driver's door,

heaved the stunned man out of the car and then dragged him to the back of the car. He popped the trunk, put the soldier inside and then slammed the lid closed.

Looking around, Herron smiled. Nobody had seen him.

He jumped into the driver's seat and quickly drove away from the Yacht Club. He guessed he had very little time to stop the transportation of the families to the prison – how long did it take to round up some supposed dissidents? Normally, he'd prepare an operation for days or weeks, then execute it flawlessly, but without all the information he needed and with little idea of the time frame, he was going to have to improvise.

Taking a left, he headed onto the main road that cut through Suva, navigating towards the supermax and the one road he could be sure a prison transport would take.

He was on the hunt.

* * *

He caught up with the Army truck eight minutes later on the outskirts of the capital, closer to the prison than he'd have preferred. He hit the gas and slowly inched closer, waiting for his chance. He'd have to play it cool because the soldiers in the truck would be alert for an attack by the Movement.

Glancing into the opposite lane, he saw only one car traveling towards him. As soon as it passed and the road was clear, he took his shot. Foot to the floor, he darted out and overtook the truck at high speed. Now in front, he merged into the truck's lane again and tapped the brakes, gradually slowing and forcing the transport to do likewise.

Deftly, he steered the car to foil any effort by the truck driver to overtake him and finally both vehicles came to a stop.

Herron unbuckled his seatbelt, opened the door and climbed out. The soldier he'd locked in the trunk was pounding and shouting to be let free, but Herron ignored him. He flashed a look of anger at the driver of the truck and held his hands wide, the universal gesture for 'What the hell are you doing?'

The driver and the soldier riding shotgun glanced at each other, clearly unsure how to handle the situation. After a few seconds of conversation, the man in the passenger seat popped his door open and climbed down. He had a scowl on his face and a pistol on his hip.

Perfect.

The guard barked something at Herron, who ignored him and walked forward, palms facing out, indicating he didn't want any trouble.

Seeing this Westerner wasn't about to halt as instructed, the guard moved to draw his weapon. Herron took the last step needed to get within reach then grabbed the man's wrist, breaking it and forcing the pistol out of his hand. Using all his strength, he pulled on the arm and the guard overbalanced, falling towards him.

Herron kneed him in the face then released him, letting him drop.

He picked up the pistol and aimed it at the driver, who hadn't managed to draw his own weapon. The

Fijian was smart. He put his hands on top of the steering wheel.

Herron gestured with his head for the driver to exit the vehicle. As soon as the Fijian soldier had climbed down from the truck, Herron pistol whipped him and he, too, dropped to the ground.

After looking in both directions to make sure no cars were coming, he went to the back of the truck and climbed up to see inside. A few dozen people stared back at him. Most looked frightened and confused, yet a few had a twinkle of curiosity in their eyes.

"You're all safe." Herron said with a smile. "The soldiers are out cold and you've got a few minutes to get out of here."

None of them moved.

"What the hell is wrong with you all?" Herron frowned. "These soldiers were taking you to Suva Prison. If you end up there, you're never getting out!"

After a few more seconds of silence, a woman spoke up. "Who're you? Why are you helping us to escape?"

"I'm the best chance you've got." Herron glanced at a few of the other prisoners. "Better than being in that hellhole."

"You're right about that," the woman said. "Dozens of people have died in that prison."

"I'm trying to spare you all that same fate, but we don't have much time. Can you drive?"

"I can."

He climbed down and opened the rear of the truck, holding out a hand for the woman. She took it, and climbed down to the ground, then headed for the front of the truck. Herron closed the back compartment again, trusting the woman to get her charges to a safe place. Fiji was small, but there were still plenty of places to hide if they were smart.

"You have my thanks." The woman settled in behind the wheel. "I wish you'd been there to help my husband the way you've have helped us."

"He's locked up in there too?"

She nodded. "Alexander Pillay. Perhaps you've heard of him?"

Herron looked at her, his face blank.

"He was well-known here for a time. A colonel in Army, before he joined the resistance and was imprisoned. If he'd known the General would come for us too…"

Her voice tailed off, tears welling in her eyes. Herron stepped back from the cab, said nothing. He'd given these people a chance. Now all he wanted to do was get the hell away from Fiji.

At last, the woman started the truck and got it moving. He watched as it disappeared into the distance then walked over to the soldiers he'd knocked out. They'd have sore heads for a week. He dug through their pockets and took their cellphones, throwing both as far as he could away from the road, one after the other. Then he returned to the car he'd been driving and ripped the radio receiver out of the dashboard.

He could've driven the car back to the Yacht Club, but it was possible the truck driver had reported its number when it had forced them to stop in the middle of the road. If so, the authorities would spot him as soon as he entered Suva. Instead, he started off down the road in the direction of the prison, hoping to hail a ride and get back to the city.

He had done as much good on the island as he could. Now it really was time to go.

* * *

Herron plastered a dumb-looking smile on his face and then waved at the beaten-up sedan that was approaching him at a speed well below the limit. Despite its glacial progress, the vehicle was his best chance to get back to Suva and off Fiji before the alert was raised and prevented his escape.

The driver stopped the car and wound down the window. "You break down?"

"Something like that." Herron figured it was best to omit the details. "Could I grab a ride?"

"Sure."

Herron felt a pang of relief as he got in and closed the door. "Thanks."

As they slowly chewed up the miles back to the city, they made small talk, the driver saying he lived in Suva, worked at the prison and liked both. Gradually the natural landscape outside the car gave way to urban development – small homes, the occasional business, better-quality roads and other public infrastructure – and Herron allowed himself to relax a little. In 15 minutes, he'd be on his boat and preparing to leave Fiji.

The driver's cellphone rang. He sighed and looked at Herron. "It's my boss."

Herron shrugged. "Do what you need to do."

The driver smiled and answered the phone.

Herron only caught one side of the conversation. It was enough.

"Yes, sir, I'm nearly home...No, I didn't see a truck..."

He turned to look at Herron.

The game was up.

The driver continued to listen to his boss, but by now he wasn't really paying attention. He was clearly computing what he should do about the stranger in his car, a man he'd clearly been told was dangerous, who'd probably just intercepted an army truck, taken out its guards, and freed its prisoners.

It was the ultimate test of duty versus self-preservation.

He hung up the phone, said nothing.

"Keep your eyes on the road." Herron tried to keep his voice calm. He didn't want to hurt the driver, a working stiff who'd just been hit with a bit of bad luck. "There's no need to be a hero."

The driver clenched the wheel tighter. "If my boss finds out you were in my car and I didn't try to take you in, I'll lose my job."

"Get a new one."

"Where?" The man shrugged, like his question had the most obvious answer in the world. "There's nothing left on Fiji that belongs to Fijians. The only jobs are with the government, the army, or the American or Chinese-owned companies. I'm too old for the army and the government, and I won't work for the foreigners who're destroying the island."

Herron sighed as the driver's eyes flicked down to the footwell. When he'd destroyed the Enclave, he'd sworn he wouldn't harm any more civilians. Now he mightn't have a choice.

"Don't." Herron spoke softly. "Please."

But the driver ignored him, reaching into the footwell to grab a pistol.

Herron snapped into action, gripping the wheel to keep it steady while using his other hand to punch the inside of the driver's elbow. The man cried out and released the wheel, letting Herron secure it.

That only left the pistol.

Herron clubbed the driver's collarbone and the man grunted in pain. He'd struggle to use the pistol now, so Herron took hold of it, keeping it aimed at the floor. After checking to see the safety was on, he wrenched the gun from its owner.

"Give it up." Herron tossed the weapon into his own footwell. He didn't want any more violence. "It's over."

"Yes, it is." The driver's voice was melancholy. "If I fail to take you in, the General will have me flayed alive..."

He floored the gas pedal and the sedan shot forward.

Before Herron could reach out to kill the ignition or pull on the handbrake, the car hit a pothole, jerking the steering wheel in his hand. The driver added to his troubles, pulling the wheel to the right and forcing Herron to struggle to stay on the road.

He failed.

With no safety barrier to stop it, the vehicle rumbled over rough terrain, heading straight for a tree. When the impact came, Herron was thrown forward. His head slammed into the dashboard. He grunted in pain.

A second later, it was over.

Gradually Herron came to his senses. The driver had hit his head on the steering wheel and was out cold.

Herron reached out to feel for a pulse. It took a moment, but he found one. The driver would live.

He fumbled for the buckle release of his seatbelt and then opened the door of the battered vehicle. He climbed out and staggered away from the car, but only made it a few steps before he registered the field they'd bumped across.

The ground was uneven, explaining the rough ride, and had the look of a building site to it – as if it had been excavated for construction, then forgotten about. Trash was scattered on the surface, and where the tires of the car had churned up the dirt, glimpses of white rocks could be seen in the soil

Still dazed and struggling to focus, Herron was right on top of the rocks before he realized what he was really seeing.

Bones.

He was standing on a mass grave.

5

BLOOD TRICKLED from a cut in his head and he was sore from the car crash, but Herron was alive. As he'd walked back to the outskirts of Suva, he'd given up on the idea of sailing away. He now had a new reason for sticking around. What had started out as saving a few civilians was now a rescue mission for an entire country.

That the General could murder so many people and then bury them in a field beside a highway was outrageous. Although he'd left the mass grave undisturbed, Herron had seen enough to be sure that he was in the middle of an island that was tearing itself apart, sinking deeper into the mire of turmoil. Innocent people were dying and desperate, betrayed by those who were supposed to lead. The General ground all opposition into dust at any sign of a threat and that instinct had cost his people dearly.

Now it'd cost the General.

As he got closer to town, he could see further signs of the General's crackdown. More troops and vehicles were on the streets, more prison trucks were being filled, and several buildings were on fire. Decimating the Movement had done nothing to stop the chaos and Fiji was quickly going to hell, no matter how hard the General tried to contain the situation.

There was only one person on the island Herron could trust, so he made his way to the man's house. Eventually, he arrived and knocked on the door. While he waited for an answer, he considered the likelihood that the occupant would help him. Ten years ago, the man had said he would be Herron's friend for life – would that extend to sheltering a wanted fugitive?

After a few moments, Herron heard deadbolts unlocking and a chain sliding back. The door opened and revealed the father of the girl Herron had saved from a pedophile so many years before. The man's mood was warm in an instant and he greeted Herron with a wide smile, despite not having seen him in a decade.

"My friend!" Jone Nath sported a wide grin. "You've returned!"

"I'm sorry to bother you, Jone," Herron replied. "I really need your help."

"Hurry!" Nath gestured for Herron to enter the house. "If the troops see you there'll be trouble."

Herron stepped inside and his benefactor closed the door and locked it again. As they made their way through to the kitchen, Herron saw it was a cozy place, filled with the usual detritus of a settled and happy family. Herron felt a pang of guilt about asking these people for help, knowing it'd expose them to danger.

Nath gestured at his wife, who was standing near the sink. "This is Veena."

It suddenly dawned on him that he'd never even

introduced himself to this family he was hoping would help him. "My name is Mitch Herron. Thank you both for welcoming me into your home."

The woman sized him up, clearly determining whether he was a threat to her family, then the penny dropped. "You're the one who saved my girl?"

Herron nodded and instantly the mood in the room grew irresistibly warm. Veena ushered him to a chair at the dining table and then began to cook. For Herron, the chance to sit and rest was welcome, but the prospect of home cooking was the rarest treasure.

As Veena prepared the meal, Herron made conversation. "Are you safe with everything going on out there?"

"Safe enough. I work in finance for the Ministry of Industry. It's an important job, so they mostly leave me alone, but Veena is often too scared to leave the house. Lynda, my daughter, is at the university studying to be a doctor, but all this has interrupted her work." He looked at Herron, then at his wife, then back to Herron. When he spoke, he chose his words carefully. "The General has done much harm."

Herron considered the statement to be a box ticked. "And the Movement? Do they stand a chance of overthrowing him and bringing in something better?"

"No." Nath shrugged. "This is the latest attempt by rabble rousers to install new leadership. It'll fail, just like the others. The General is an expert at crushing his enemies and putting fear into the populace."

Herron nodded. The General had become top dog by resisting and then beating the *former* top dog, who'd been in power for twenty years. It was unsurprising no individual or group had been strong enough to topple him, especially since modern technology made it easier than ever to surveil resistance and destroy it when it became a problem.

Luckily, men like Herron could still be effective, even against modern technology.

Herron looked at Nath. "I want to remove the General from power and make the streets safe for your family."

Nath shook his head. "That's a lofty ambition, my friend. But unfortunately, the General isn't the whole story..."

The General and his regime hadn't always been so bad, Nath told him. They'd been a little overbearing, but the people had largely been left alone. There'd been jobs – mostly in tourism and industries backed by American multinationals – and life had been good. There hadn't been enough tension to warrant a challenge to the status quo.

Then the gas had been discovered and foreign-owned companies had arrived on the island.

As the Chinese company had asserted themselves, they'd started to butt heads with American interests the government had aligned with. The General and his administration had been ill-equipped to handle the conflict and a few months ago he'd attempted to expel the Chinese. At about the same time, the trouble with the Movement had started and now the General had declared martial law.

Herron frowned as Nath finished his story, the situation now clearer in his mind. "So, one company is propping up the General and another is propping up the Movement?"

"Yes. And both sides will do anything to win. There's

a lot of money at stake since they found the gas. Stopping one side or the other won't be enough to bring change."

Herron nodded. It was a scenario as old as time, resource wars fought by proxy. "Then they all need to go. I need information about the companies – what they own and who their key people are..."

"I work for the bureaucracy. That'll be simple. But first, you can eat something and meet the girl you saved so many years ago."

* * *

As automatic gunfire sounded far in the distance, Herron looked at Lynda and was surprised to see she didn't react at all. It seemed, like most Fijians, she'd become used to the daily violence and carnage.

"We should head inside," he said, and gestured in the direction of the back door. "It's not safe for you to be outside."

"It's not safe anywhere. I won't be a prisoner in my home." She wrinkled her nose. "The General's thugs get you, the Movement's thugs get you – it's all the same."

"I hope to change that." He found it troubling such a young woman – in her early twenties and at the start of her life – should be so weary with the world. It strengthened his resolve to fix the problem.

"Doesn't matter. I'm getting away from Fiji as soon as I've saved up enough money. I want to go to America or Europe to practice medicine."

Getting away seemed to be her thing. Soon after meeting Herron in the family kitchen, she'd asked him to accompany her into the back yard. With the blessing of her parents, he'd agreed, and when they'd finished their meal they'd headed outside. It had been clear she'd wanted to get something off her chest.

When he didn't respond immediately, she continued. "I remember what happened, you know."

"When?"

"When you stopped that creep from raping me. I didn't even know your name, but I've never forgotten you. I actually think about you a lot."

Herron's instincts flared and he leaned back, even as she closed her eyes and leaned in to kiss him. When she realized he was no longer there, she opened her eyes and stared at him. Then, her face clouded over with confusion.

He sighed and followed. "That can't happen, Lynda."

She didn't respond.

"You're barely twenty years old."

She flared. "Yes! I am! And that's old enough to choose!"

"Sure, but I can choose not to."

She looked at him for a long time, seemingly waiting for him to change his mind. She wasn't used to not getting her way. He could understand why. She was a good-looking and almost six-feet tall, but the intensity of her eyes was where it all started and ended, a vortex that pulled you in and wouldn't let you go.

She'd make someone very happy one day.

She deserved to be happy too.

It was Herron that broke the silence. "Forget about me, finish university, get a cool job, find a lover."

Her features lightened a little. Although she was still clearly hurt and unhappy, she leaned in to kiss him on the cheek. He didn't back away this time, recognizing that the mood and her intent had changed into something he found acceptable.

He changed the topic, trying to move on from her strange infatuation with him. "So you're studying to be a doctor?"

"Not yet." She rolled her eyes. "My father exaggerates, but when I finish my undergraduate degree, I want to study medicine in America. Or Europe. I have the grades to do it, but not the money."

Herron let the statement lie, although a plan was forming in his head. Once he'd rid the island of its tyrannical leadership and the companies that contributed to the problem, he'd return and see if he could take care of Lynda and her family. It seemed the least he could do for Nath's family after they'd sheltered him and it'd help give their daughter the start she deserved.

His train of thought was derailed by an explosion off in the distance. They looked at each other, then towards the sound, and a few seconds later greasy brown smoke rose into the sky. Somewhere, a building was on fire.

"I need to talk to your father." Herron stood from the chair he was sitting in. "We'll speak again."

"I hope so." She smiled, but made no move to rise herself. "Good luck."

Herron nodded and walked back inside the house, finding Nath in the kitchen. "What happened?"

"It was the Council of Chiefs complex." He spoke the words solemnly, as if something of great value had been destroyed. "The Government is already broadcasting a name they say is responsible."

Herron snorted. "Let me guess..."

"They're claiming you're responsible." Nath finished Herron's thought for him. "You need to come inside. If they find you on the street, they'll shoot first and ask questions later."

Herron nodded. The remnants of the Movement or its mercenary allies had attacked Suva again. They were probably trying to punish the General for his crackdown, but Herron knew it'd only mean to more misery for the citizens of Suva. Caught between two warring sides, they were taking the worst of the violence.

And now the General was taking the opportunity to blame him for it.

"You're welcome to stay for as long as you need to," Veena said. "Or return as often as you like."

"No. I need to get out of here. I'm going to take care of the General, the Movement and the warring companies." He drew the pistol he'd taken from the prison guard's car and held it out for them. "In the meantime, this will keep you safe."

Nath looked at the weapon, but he made no move to take it. "We've never owned a gun and don't plan to now."

Herron shifted his gaze to Veena. Without saying a word, she dried her hands and took the pistol. He spent a minute talking her through how to use it, then she stashed the weapon at the top of the tallest kitchen cupboard.

"Thank you." She cast a glance at her husband that dared him to object. It was clear she was the leader of the house.

"Now." Herron turned to Nath. "Where's this Chinese gas company operate from?"

"They have an office in Suva and their extraction facility in Nadi," Nath said. "I looked into it while you were out walking."

"I'll go to Nadi," Herron said. "Less heat on me there."

Nath paused, glanced at his wife, then looked back at Herron. "Take our car. It's reliable and will get you there without any trouble."

Herron shook his head. "I can't do that. I—"

"I won't have it any other way." Nath held up a hand. "Saving our girl was worth a lifetime of cars. Dealing with the General and the Movement would be worth a second lifetime."

Herron was ready to argue, but the looks on their faces sealed the deal. They'd already given him so much – food, rest, information – and now they wanted to give him more. They wanted this to be their contribution to righting the wrongs on Fiji.

"All right. Thank you."

Sometime later, after Nath had talked Herron through his findings about both the US and Chinese companies, the whole family accompanied Herron outside. The chaos of wailing sirens, speeding emergency vehicles and panicked cries had subsided a little. Nath showed him to the car and Herron climbed inside, winding the window down to say his goodbyes. Then, finally, he hit the road.

It was time to get back to business.

6

HERRON SIGHED as he climbed out of the car and stretched his legs. It had been a four-hour drive from Suva to Nadi and he'd stuck to the Queens Road the entire way, which hugged the coast on the south side of the island and offered some of the best scenery anywhere in the world. He hadn't stopped to enjoy the views, though. He had work to do.

The main street of Nadi was bustling with a different sort of activity to the capital – tourists enjoying their downtime and locals going about their day. Overall, it seemed a little less chaotic than Suva. He regretted that he was about to unleash a wave of destruction, shattering the peace, but it had to happen to end the civil war. Because it was here that the China National Offshore Gas Corporation had the bulk of its operations.

He'd rehearsed the plan in his head during the long drive. Reaching into the car, he grabbed a bag of stuff he'd purchased from a roadside shack that sold all manner of tourist-trap trinkets. He pulled out a baseball cap and put it on his head, then tied a dishcloth around his neck and pulled it up over his face. Both items were printed with 'I love Fiji'.

It wasn't a masterful disguise, but it'd do the job.

He crossed the street and headed for the ANZ Bank branch. There was a guard outside and he made a beeline toward him. The security man didn't even look up from his cellphone until Herron was almost on top of him. Then, panicking as he saw the masked man approaching, he reached for his pistol.

Herron punted him in the balls before he could draw it.

The guard crumpled to the ground. Herron took his pistol, walked straight into the bank, and fired a shot into the air. Chaos erupted. Some people froze and some people screamed, but all of them quickly realized who was in charge.

"Get on the ground and you'll live!" As others complied, he aimed the pistol at a teller. "Not you."

"Please don't hurt me!" The woman was frozen in place. "You need—"

"I need money!" Herron stepped closer to the counter and aimed the pistol at the shocked woman's head. "Now!"

As she lowered a trembling hand towards the till and out of sight, he knew exactly what she was planning to do. A second later, security screens shot up from the counters, separating the public floor from the teller area. Stealing the bank's cash would be very difficult now.

"Damn it!" He fired a few more shots into the ceiling. "Nobody move for the next 10 minutes!"

He fled back to his car and burned rubber away

from the bank, pushing the vehicle to its limits. Somewhere between Suva and Nadi, he'd removed the license plates, because he didn't want Nath and his family to get in trouble. But he still had to evade the cops for his plan to work.

Pedestrians stared at the car as it blazed past them. Within a minute, he turned down a side road and then doubled back, heading in the direction of the bank he'd just robbed. Soon, he pulled into a parking lot, removed the cap and dishcloth, and changed his shirt. Then he left the car and walked back to the main street.

Herron relaxed as he walked. The cops would be swarming on the bank, looking for a guy in a car wearing an 'I love Fiji' disguise. They certainly wouldn't expect their suspect to return to the scene of the crime. Now Herron was just one American among dozens in the area and he'd be long gone before the cops figured out who they were after.

Police sirens wailed, blue lights flashing in the distance. Herron smiled. He'd counted on this response. He'd never intended to take a dime from the bank, he'd just needed the attempted robbery to act as a lightning rod, drawing police manpower away from his true target.

He had more valuable treasure than money in mind and now the cops had left it unguarded.

He strolled along the main street, took a left and headed for the Nadi Police Station. He entered the station and made his way to the front reception. A cop was behind the counter, listening intently to his police radio. The bank job was probably the most exciting thing to happen in Nadi for a decade and this guy was probably upset to be missing it.

Herron cleared his throat and pressed on the little bell on the counter. "I need a moment of your time."

"What is it, sir?" The cop's voice had an edge.

Herron guffawed, deliberately hamming it up to cheese off the officer. "I want to report a stolen beach rug."

"A...what?" The cop frowned and stood, staring at Herron as if he couldn't believe what he was hearing. "Sir, the bank was just robbed..."

"You won't help me?" Herron leaned against the counter and got in the cop's face. "What kind of service is that for a visitor to your country?"

"Sir, you need to back off. I—"

Herron drew the pistol he'd stolen from the security guard and aimed it at him. "Be cool."

The cop's eyes widened. "I—"

"Hand over your weapon."

"Okay." The officer reached down, took the pistol from its holster and placed it on the counter.

Herron picked it up. "Now show me where the arms locker is."

The man nodded and Herron followed him through the station. They reached an area not accessible by the public, a mix of offices and storage rooms. Against the wall at the end of the corridor was a six-foot-tall steel cabinet with a keypad lock.

"This is it," the officer said. "Please reconsider. I—"

"Open it."

Herron kept a close eye on the cop as he punched numbers into the digital keypad. This was the moment of truth. If the he entered the code correctly, Herron would have all the guns he needed. If he didn't, all this effort would be for naught.

The light on the keypad switched from red to green.

Herron smiled. "Now you're going to walk me to the cells."

Nervously, the cop did as he was told, and Herron nudged him inside one of the cages, locking the door behind him. The cop had been cooperative and Herron was glad the only consequence for him would be a little professional humiliation.

He returned to the unlocked cabinet, opened the door and grinned.

He'd found the motherlode.

Taking his time, he inspected the contents of the cabinet. Inside were pistols, shotguns and submachine guns – plenty of options for up-close-and-personal work. More intriguing were the long guns: scoped rifles for use by trained snipers. Herron was surprised to find those inside a regular police station.

It seemed Fijian cops liked to be prepared for anything.

Herron assembled his arsenal: a couple of pistols and a silenced submachine gun, a scoped rifle, and some flashbang and tear gas grenades. A quick search turned up a cop's gym bag; Herron emptied out its contents, and stuffed everything except the rifle inside.

The most dangerous man in Fiji now had the most firepower, too.

* * *

Herron took a pull of his beer and kept his eyes down, not wanting to attract casual interest or conversation from the hotel barman or the other guests. It was a nice place, with a bar running the length of the room and a mix of tables and sofas covering the rest of the floor. Hanging out there made a nice change of pace from fighting on the streets and being on the run. It was also the key to furthering his plan.

Since acquiring his supply of weapons, Herron had spent some time online, adding to the research Nath had done for him in Suva. It left him with one iron-clad conclusion: the largest US natural gas company and its Chinese state-owned competitor had a history of turf wars. Both corporations bribed and coerced politicians, ignored laws and regulations, and aggressively protected their interests.

Ending the civil war wasn't a matter of threatening one person, or bringing another to justice, or even taking out a couple of troublemakers. Stopping the madness would require stripping the country's politics and economy back to their foundations, because Fiji was caught between immensely powerful interests.

Interests that weren't used to losing.

To get the General out, he'd have to get them out, and China National were first on his list. He had the proof he needed to convince himself that was the right course of action and an arsenal of weapons with which to finish the job, but he didn't yet know *how* to do that. The key to finding out was a meeting with the head of the Chinese company's local operation, a Ms Yang.

Nath had told him that although Ms Yang lived in Fiji now, she'd chosen to live in this hotel rather than a house of her own. Herron guessed she'd almost certainly appear in the hotel bar at some point, and he was sure happy to wait. His former careers in the military and as a contract killer had taught him patience. There were times he'd spent days in the mud, looking down a scope and waiting for a target, eating and pissing in the same spot, until he got the shot

A warm, comfortable bar was nothing in comparison.

It was only another hour before Ms Yang walked in. A tall woman, she cut an impressive figure, wearing a navy pantsuit with a cream-colored silk blouse, and walking on pumps that probably cost more than Herron's yacht. While she'd doubtless been at work all day, she looked as fresh as morning.

He watched as she took a seat at the bar. She ordered and the barman quickly delivered her red wine and the check. She signed for the drink, took a sip and looked around, her eyes sliding over Herron without stopping. She was clearly looking for someone in particular.

An immense hatred coursed through him at the thought of the woman responsible for the Movement and their mercenary allies relaxing with a glass of merlot, oblivious to the blood on her hands. He had just as much ill-feeling for the General and the American company that propped him up, but he'd compartmentalized that for another day.

For now, all his attention was on Ms Yang.

She sat alone for a while, drinking and checking her cellphone, then a Fijian man entered and headed straight for her. Herron's eyes narrowed as the man took the seat beside her, reached into his pocket for a folded piece of paper and placed it on the bar. This done, he departed, and Ms Yang put the paper in her purse.

Herron almost laughed. It was the most amateur exchange he'd ever seen. And now he wanted to know what the man had given her.

He waited until Ms Yang stood up to leave, then drained his beer and gave the bartender the universal gesture for 'pour me another' – a half-clenched hand gripping an imaginary glass, tilted up and down a few times. The bartender complied, giving Herron the opening he needed.

Herron put some money on the bar and took his beer, as he did so glancing down at the check Ms Yang had signed. Now he had her room number.

It really was amateur hour.

He returned to his seat, sipped on his beer for a few minutes, then slipped out of the bar. He hoped by now Ms Yang was settled in for the night, running a bath or getting ready for bed. She'd had a long day, after all.

Arriving at her room, he knocked softly, the sort of knock an apologetic hotel staffer would make, embarrassed to be disturbing a guest. Footsteps shuffled on the other side of the door.

"Who is it?" Yang sounded annoyed. "This had better be important."

"Sorry to disturb you, miss. I work in the hotel bar. The bill..."

The door opened and an irritated Ms Yang peered out. "What do you—?"

Herron stepped forward, slamming the door against her. She let out a cry of surprise, but he was already inside, closing the door behind him. He gripped her blouse firmly and pulled her deeper into the room, before throwing her down roughly on the sofa, drawing his pistol from the waistband of his shorts and aiming it at her.

"You're a very stupid man." She smiled, her teeth

flawless. She didn't seem panicked at all by the situation. "You don't know who you're dealing with."

Herron pressed the pistol against her forehead. "Let me try my knowledge for size."

Despite the gun, her eyes twinkled in amusement. "Okay."

"Your government wants control of Fiji's natural gas reserves, but you don't like that the American competition has the General in their pocket. Good so far?"

She nodded.

"You decided to contest the situation by resourcing locals who want change. You supply the Movement with weapons and information. In return, when they take over, you get exclusive access."

Another nod.

"Unfortunately, they proved to be insufficient, so you called in the cavalry – mercenaries. Now hundreds of Fijians have died and life on the island has become a misery for pretty much everyone."

"Not bad." She raised an eyebrow. "Although I don't know what this little display is meant to achieve. You're up against two warring sides, supported by powerful companies, backed by two great powers. Breaking into my room and threatening me gets you nowhere. I'm a cog in a machine, simply doing my job. If not me, it'll be someone else."

"You're right." Herron laughed. "*This* little display mightn't achieve much, but blowing up your pumping station will…"

She stared at him as if he was crazy. "That's impossible. It's one of the most well-guarded facilities on Fiji."

"Oh, you'd be surprised..." Herron shrugged. "All I need from you is an answer to one very simple question: How do I blow it up once I'm inside?"

She blinked in apparent confusion, then shook her head. "I know nothing about how the facility actually works. I'm a party appointee. I barely ever even visit the pumping station..."

Anger rose up inside Herron again. He believed her. She had no answers. Yang's power derived from her position. She had no particular technical or business expertise that'd give him the answers he needed to plan his next move.

With a sigh, he changed his plans on the fly. While he'd hoped she was an expert that would've given him the key to destroying the facility, it was clear she was just a mouthpiece. He'd have to figure out the facility himself. Thankfully, he was good at improvising.

But first, there was the matter of his prisoner and her secret slip of paper.

Keeping the gun trained on her, he considered ending her life. But if he rendered her organization's position on Fiji untenable, then she'd be rendered inert anyway, forced to return to China to meet whatever punishment her angry masters decided to mete out.

Adding another body to Fiji's civil war would just bring more heat down upon him.

His mind made up, he kept the gun trained on her, walked to her wardrobe and rifled the drawers. He found several pairs of pantyhose and forced her to tie her feet together. Then he bound her wrists and hogtied them to her ankles. Once he was finished, she was as helpless as a newborn.

"I suggest you take a deep breath," he said, and stuffed a cushion cover into her mouth.

He'd spotted Ms Yang's purse while searching her wardrobe and retrieved the piece of paper. He unfolded it and glanced at her. The look on her face told him all he needed to know. Although he'd had all the proof he needed before, now he had it in writing.

"You motherfuckers." He shot her a look of the darkest disdain. "You evil motherfuckers."

He was going to burn her corporation to the ground.

7

HERRON WHISTLED SOFTLY as he picked through the bag of firearms, choosing his tools for the job. He hung two of the submachine guns over his shoulder by their straps, stuck another pistol in the waistband of his shorts and hefted the rifle in his hands. He finished his loadout with ammo, two flashbangs and two tear gas grenades.

Satisfied he had enough to eradicate the Chinese company's presence on the island, he threw the bag containing the rest of his weapons into some bushes and then slammed the trunk of his stolen car. He could come back for the guns later, once his target was a smoldering ruin. He doubted he'd be able to do the same with the car.

If all went to plan, its owner would have a compelling insurance claim.

He took a second to glance up at the processing plant, a hundred yards ahead of him. It was a giant facility, easily the tallest and most impressive structure he'd seen on the island. Natural gas was pumped from it onto ships berthed alongside – they simply sucked up their fill of the liquid gold and then sailed off to deliver it to China.

Not for long.

The paper he'd extracted from Ms Yang's purse had been a manifest for weapons for the Movement – hidden and shipped in on a tanker – and a payment and deployment schedule for the mercenaries her company had hired. Most recently, that deployment had included blowing up the Council of Tribal Chiefs complex.

Elsewhere in her room, he'd found details of an aggressive expansion of their campaign, which would target dozens of civilian sites and likely result in hundreds of casualties. It was an escalation that Herron wouldn't allow to happen. China National, the mercenaries and the Movement were cancers on the local populace every bit as bad as the General.

He saw only one way to get the corporation off the island – a devastating attack on this facility, causing so much damage it'd be too resource-intensive to rebuild. Without the gas resources, they'd likely stop paying the mercenaries and propping up the resistance. It wouldn't take care of all the island's problems, but it'd be a start.

He opened the gas tank of the car and inserted a rag far enough that only the end was sticking out. When he was finished, he got back behind the wheel, racked the seat forward, started the car, and wedged one of his submachine guns between the bottom of the seat and the gas pedal.

The engine turned over and revved hard, but the car stayed in place, the handbrake engaged and the vehicle in park. Next, he returned to the gas tank and used his zippo to light the rag. When it was burning satisfactorily, he pocketed the lighter and sat back in the driver's seat with his legs hanging out of the open door.

He disengaged the handbrake and then shifted the vehicle into drive. "Time to go loud."

Freed of its restraints, the car kicked forward and gained speed, heading for the front gate of the facility. Herron remained in the car until he was sure everything was going to plan, then jumped out. He rolled, climbed to his feet and ran into the scrub on the side of the road to retrieve his backpack and rifle.

Crouched down in the roadside foliage, he watched the car tear straight towards the facility, the rag in the gas tank burning furiously. The two guards manning the front gates had stepped onto the road, one holding his hand out and ordering the vehicle to stop, the other taking aim with his pistol.

When the car was thirty yards out, the second guard started to fire on it...

It kept coming.

Fifteen yards out, and his comrade joined in, peppering the front of the vehicle with rounds...

The car didn't stop.

Both men jumped out of the way just before the sedan plowed into the gate. Despite an awesome crash, the steel-framed barrier held, stopping the car dead. Its wheels continued to spin and the rag in the gas tank continued to burn, creating a strange contest as to which would go first: the gate or the gas tank.

The gas tank won.

A fireball blossomed above the vehicle and a roar

assaulted his ears. The force of the explosion sent the two guards flying and also finished what the collision had started, dislodging the gate from its rails and knocking it over.

Herron lifted the rifle to his shoulder and stared down its scope. He could now see deeper into the facility and the results of the frontal assault were impressive. As the car continued to burn, red lights were flashing and guards were scrambling everywhere, some of them searching for the threat and others searching for safety.

Herron aimed at a man who was rushing towards the burning car with a shotgun in his hand. He didn't want to slaughter the mercenaries employed to protect the facility, but they had too many men and too much firepower for any other approach. He pulled the trigger, and the man dropped.

From this range, it was like shooting fish in a barrel. He fired every few seconds and had taken three of the mercenaries out before anyone inside the base knew what was happening. He downed two more as they scrambled and shouted at each other to find cover.

Once they had, it became a stalemate.

Herron continued to look through the rifle scope, waiting for a shot. He didn't get one. The defenders had smartened up and were starving him of targets. While he didn't think the cops or the army would be racing to the rescue, given the General's opposition to the Chinese company, he also didn't think he'd have the time to wait the mercenaries out. When the benefit of shock and surprise wore off, the soldiers would realize they had numerical superiority and adapt.

He took the magazine out of the rifle and pocketed

it. The rifle was harmless without its ammo, so he tossed it into the bushes. He swapped to the submachine gun, climbed to his feet and advanced on the gate. He moved quickly, knowing he only had a few more seconds before one of the defenders realized there was no more rifle fire incoming.

He closed to fifty yards before the first mercenary dared to stick his head out from cover. Herron levelled the submachine gun and fired a long burst at him. The shots blew the mercenary's head into a bloody mess. Leaving spent shell casings in his wake, Herron continued forward, firing burst after burst, keeping his foes suppressed.

When he was twenty yards out, the defenders started to return fire with some level of coordination. Herron dived to the ground and grunted as he landed, relying on the darkness and his low profile to keep him safe. He was now close enough to the gate and the fence that he could commence stage two of his plan.

As shots sailed over his head, he grabbed three of the grenades he'd stashed on his combat webbing – one flashbang and two tear gas. One-by-one, he pulled the pins on the grenades and tossed them over the fence of the facility. The *pop-pop-pop* of the pistols the mercenaries were packing continued to enliven the night, but it was nothing compared to the impact of the grenades.

The result was deafening noise, blinding flashes and eye-stinging gas. The gunfire stopped as some of the defenders retreated deeper into the facility, giving up on their attempt to hold him off, and rolling out the welcome mat.

Herron climbed to his feet and advanced.

The wounded were out of action, aside from their screams of pain.

The dead made no sound at all.

Only one mercenary hadn't retreated from the gate area. He was heavily affected by the tear gas, clutching at his eyes and firing blind with his pistol, so Herron had no choice but to put him down. He fired a burst from his submachine gun and the man dropped, giving Herron control of the entrance to the facility.

He crouched down behind a parked mercenary vehicle and swapped out his magazine. The firefight to pry open the entrance had burned through much of his ammunition, but he had enough to finish the job. When he was good to go, he peered up from behind cover and considered his next move.

From the gate area, the natural gas depot split off into three distinct areas. The main game was the pumping station, which dominated the rest of the facility. It had large steel pipes that disappeared into the ground and into the ocean, above which there was a superstructure of towering gantries. To the left of it were administration buildings and to the right was the dock.

He moved from cover, advancing fast and low, his eyes searching for new targets. Although the defenders at the gate had been armed with pistols, it was possible the mercenaries had posted riflemen on the gantries.

That would've been Herron's second line of defense, if he was in charge.

He made it to the base of the gantry that covered the pumping station before he was challenged again. A defender was in cover behind a steel pillar. Herron pushed on, unleashing several short bursts of fire at the pillar while he closed in, making sure his foe stayed pinned.

When Herron had closed to within one hundred yards – no distance at all for a submachine gun – the mercenary tried his luck, spinning from behind cover and firing his pistol. Herron kept moving, trusting his skill and range advantage.

He fired a burst and cut the mercenary down, then continued on to the gantry.

While he couldn't see any more enemies, Herron knew they were close. He could hear the pounding of their footsteps on the walkway and soon more would converge from the other areas of the depot. Now the remaining defenders had realized his target, they'd leave their positions to attack him here.

He looked around. He didn't know how to destroy the pumping facility, but he'd need to find out quickly. With no obvious place to start, he headed inside. He made it four steps before he heard a noise to his left, shifted his aim and saw a Fijian in a hard-hat.

Herron aimed his weapon at the stranger. "Who're you?"

The Fijian wasn't cowered by the submachine gun; he was braver than the mercenaries, that was for damn sure. "I work maintenance."

"Get out of here."

"I can't. I can't let you do this."

"You can't stop me." Herron waited for the man to flee, then sighed. "The company that runs this facility is killing civilians and destroying your country."

"I know that! I hope they burn in hell!" The worker's voice was firm. "But there's over a hundred civilian workers inside the facility right now!"

Herron raised an eyebrow. He hadn't noticed any sign of civilian workers and hadn't been banking on a night shift. "Where?"

The man pointed up. "The protocol for an external security breach is for non-security staff to go to the top of the gantry, while the guards shoot anything that moves down below."

"Well, they need to leave, because this place is going to blow sky-high."

The maintenance man stared at Herron for just a second. "Who're you? Are you from American Oil and Gas?"

"No. Once I'm done here, American Oil and Gas is next."

The Fijian man's eyes narrowed, and he seemed to make a decision. "My name is Niko. I'd like to help you."

"You'd do that?"

Niko laughed. "They work us for 15 hours per day and pay us almost nothing. These companies are raping Fiji, stealing our wealth and corrupting our politics. You bet I want to help you, man."

Herron considered Niko's words for a moment, then lowered his gun. "Okay. We don't have much time. We need to clear out the civilians and then figure out how to blow this facility."

"I can help with both." Niko smiled, clearly more relieved now he didn't have a gun pointed at him. He gestured to something behind Herron. "That'll take care of the first part."

Herron hesitated, not wanting to fall for the oldest trick in the book. He took a few steps back, glanced over his shoulder quickly and then looked back at Niko. He'd given it 50/50 that the Fijian was trying to distract him, but Niko hadn't moved an inch.

Herron looked behind him again and spotted what looked like a fire-alarm system on the wall. "That'll clear out the civilians?"

"The only rule that overrides the external security protocol is that alarm, because it means there's a problem with the natural gas lines. If it sounds, everyone gets out, no matter what."

Herron used the stock of his gun to smash the glass that covered the alarm panel and then pulled on the red handle inside.

The results were immediate and spectacular. Klaxons emitted an ear-piercing wail, red alarm lights flashed at regular intervals throughout the facility and a stern voice boomed over the loudspeaker.

"All personnel, evacuate immediately!"

"It'll only take a few minutes." Niko said. "Follow me. I'll take you to the facility's main control panel. We can finish the job there."

Herron nodded and followed. He could hear people running down the stairs of the gantry above him, but he couldn't see any threats as he scanned his surroundings.

They passed giant steel storage tanks and large heavy-duty hoses, until they finally reached an enclosed area with computer terminals and instrument displays.

The nerve center of the operation.

Herron looked at Niko. "Do what you need to do, but be quick about it. I'm not sure if the mercenaries defending this place will send for help."

Niko took a seat at a terminal. "I'm going to override the flow regulator and overwhelm the pipes. It'll blow the place sky high."

Herron let him go to work. He'd been planning to improvise a way to blow the facility but this was much better.

Niko's hands danced across the keyboard. A minute passed, then two, then he looked up at Herron with a satisfied expression on his face.

"It's done?"

"It's done."

"Okay, get out of here. You head down in another direction. They can't know you helped me."

Niko got out of his chair and headed for the door. "Good luck."

* * *

Herron reached the bottom of the superstructure at the same time as the more mercenaries arrived from other parts of the facility. He cursed and scrambled for cover as they fired, the bullets from their pistols ricocheting off metal. He'd hoped to get a little further before encountering resistance, but it looked like he'd need to make his stand here.

He sheltered behind a steel column as the mercenaries continued to expend their ammunition at an impressive rate, hitting nothing and achieving little except a lot of noise. Despite the futility of their attacks and the lack of damage they were causing, Herron had a sense of urgency.

The facility was going to blow, whether he was still inside it or not.

He tried to go on the offensive more than once, but each time he was met with furious gunfire. Although the mercenaries were at the maximum effective range for their pistols – about 70 yards or so – eventually one of them might get lucky. He fired a few bursts of SMG fire in response, unsure that he'd hit anything.

As shots pinged against his cover like hailstones on a roof, Herron looked around for some sort of edge. He'd faced a career of situations like this, yet there was no obvious solution this time. His mind processed every possible option in milliseconds.

He couldn't go on the offensive, because he didn't have the firepower.

He couldn't call for help, because he didn't know a soul within miles.

He couldn't wait it out, because the facility was going to blow.

He was screwed.

He was going to die in the explosion.

China National would be removed from Fiji, but the General wouldn't. Herron's mission would be only half finished, but if he was going to go down, he'd go down fighting.

Ready to make his final stand, Herron heard the throaty roar of a V8 engine getting closer. A Hummer stopped in the middle of the no man's land between him and the mercenary shooters. It was hard to understand why, until the rear driver-side window lowered and a carbine poked out.

The heavy firepower had arrived.

Herron ducked back behind cover a split-second before the carbine fired, the chatter of automatic weapon fire overwhelming. Rounds ricocheted off the pillar, but the shooter stopped firing as soon as Herron was out of sight. He was clearly more ammo conscious than his colleagues in the yard.

Herron and the merc in the Hummer engaged in a dangerous dance. Every time he tried to round from cover, the mercenary's fire would drive him back, though none of his shots found their way into flesh. Herron's mind raced, calculating roughly how many shots the frugal shooter had fired.

He reached into his pocket and pulled out his last remaining grenade, the flashbang he'd kept in reserve. He'd only have one chance to escape the situation, so execution would be vital. He waited for his moment, when there was a break in the gunshots...

...then burst into action.

Running towards the Hummer, he pulled the pin and tossed the flashbang grenade at the open rear window. He'd caught the shooter changing out his magazine, the men inside the vehicle helpless against the attack. The grenade exploded, blinding and deafening the occupants.

Herron's ears rang a little from the noise, but he'd been spared the worst of it. He rose back to his feet and approached the vehicle, keeping its bulk between himself and the other mercenaries. When he reached the window, he put two bullets into the rear shooter and then stuck his gun inside the open window and finished off the driver, who slumped onto the horn.

In five seconds, he'd flipped an impossible situation on its head.

As the horn blared and pistol shots pounded into the Hummer, Herron reached inside and unlocked the driver's door. He opened it, pulled the driver from the vehicle and dumped him on the ground, then climbed inside. Blood had sprayed over the dash, but the engine was running and once he'd locked himself in and closed the rear window, he was safe.

The mercenaries outside were still firing at the vehicle, some shots ringing harmlessly on metal and others hitting bulletproof glass, unable to damage either.

The men were doomed and they didn't even know it yet.

Herron turned the vehicle around and then floored it. The V8 engine responded with a roar, propelling him toward the main gate. The mercenaries climbed into their own vehicles and gave chase. They wouldn't catch him, though. They were soldiers of fortune. They fought for a paycheck, not for a cause. The second the heat was turned up, they melted.

And they didn't know how much heat there was about to be.

Unless some stray mercenary had found what Niko had started and knew how to stop it, nothing would prevent the facility from being blown to pieces.

Herron flashed past the main gate and hit the road. It was dark and silent, although not for much longer. When the facility eventually went up in flames, he wondered if the fire department would send help at all. They were paid by the government – the General – so they'd probably just let the place burn to the ground.

He drove for two minutes along the winding coastal roads, glancing every few seconds in his rear-vision mirror. As more time passed, he worried a stray mercenary *had* found the countdown. Then an almighty flash of light appeared in his mirrors, followed a second later by an earth-shattering explosion and a rolling fireball that climbed high into the sky.

Herron slowed the vehicle enough so he could watch, but not enough that the mercenaries would catch him. After an explosion of that size, whatever hadn't instantly been turned to slag would be worthless. He just hoped Niko and all the civilians had managed to evacuate in time.

China National was out of business.

8

HERRON SLOWED the Hummer to a stop and killed the engine, silencing the boxy vehicle. As far as he knew, the only Hummers on Fiji belonged to the mercenaries. Suva was a no-go zone for them and driving a Hummer into the city would be like a moving neon sign marking him as a target. He'd be going the rest of the way on foot.

Back in Suva, he'd move on to the next stage of the job. He'd chosen to take China National out of the picture first because they had just one interest on the island – the natural gas facility. Now it was gone, the company's interest in Fiji would blow away like sand in a cyclone, taking them and their mercenaries off the board. Starved of resources and support, the Movement would follow.

And with them out of the way, he was ready for his final showdown with the General.

The Fijian leader was another beast entirely. His corrupt roots went far deeper. He controlled the army and the police, his cronies occupied all positions of power and he was backed by a powerful American corporation that was sucking Fiji's resources dry. His troops were in the streets and his control was absolute.

Dealing with such a noxious weed would be difficult. The General would keep Fiji in his grip until his dying breath, which created a strategic problem for Herron. He didn't have enough weaponry to wipe out all the baddies, so he ruled that out. A precision hit on the General might work, but then another candidate would likely take his place, replacing one dictator with another.

No, this problem would be like surgery. He needed to slice out the infection from Fiji and then cauterize the wound so it couldn't turn rotten again. But before he could do that he needed to rest and, for that, he only had one option open to him.

He snaked his way through the streets of Suva, avoiding security checkpoints and making steady progress towards his target. With the darkness that was his only ally retreating, he picked up the pace and soon made it to Nath's house.

When he reached the house, he pounded on the door. It opened a crack and he was soon staring into the barrel of the pistol he'd left behind.

"I need to get inside." He scanned the street, expecting a patrol to appear at any moment. "I need your help one more time, my friend."

He breathed a sigh of relief as the gun barrel disappeared and the door opened fully. Nath was in the doorway, one hand urgently waving Herron inside and the other holding the pistol. Herron wondered how bad things must've got for him to be ready to use the gun he had so recently refused. Further down the hall, Veena was standing with a kitchen knife in her hand, the second line of defense. They both looked stressed and on edge.

"China National has been taken care of." He stepped inside. "Their facility is a smoldering ruin and their mercenaries have no reason to continue to support the Movement."

He followed Veena through to the kitchen, while Nath locked the door behind them. A moment later, all of them were seated around the kitchen table, just like the previous day. This time, though, the mood was far more tense. Something had changed here, more than the unrest outside.

Nath looked at his wife and then at Herron, finally revealing the source of the added tension. "While you were gone, the authorities came here and took Lynda."

Herron's eyes hardened. "Why?"

"Collusion with enemies of the state. It's clear they linked you to us and now my family is being punished."

Herron considered Nath's words for a moment. "The General didn't take you because he needs you to do your job. Taking your daughter keeps you working, but it also keeps you in line."

"So what do we do?"

Herron gave a bitter laugh. "I take down the American company, then the General, and then get your daughter back.

"How can we help?"

This family, Herron thought. They'd risked so much to help him destroy the regime squeezing the life out of Fiji, but now their daughter's safety was at stake and still they wanted to do their part.

"There's one thing. Tell me about your day job..."

* * *

Herron exited the cab and waited on the sidewalk while Nath took care of the fare. Although the streets were deserted around the Ministry of Industry building, he knew there were enough troops in the capital to make any moment of respite fleeting. Any second, a patrol could round the corner and take interest in them, so they needed to get out of the open.

Herron looked at Nath as the taxi drove off. "This is your last chance to back out."

Nath shook his head. "This building is the most secure in all of Fiji. You won't get inside without my help. And if you don't get inside, you don't get what you need to destroy the Americans."

"Most secure building in Fiji?" Herron gestured up and down the street. "They've got a funny way of showing it. There's no guards."

"There doesn't need to be." Nath's voice was full of fear. "Everyone's so afraid of the Internal Security Force that they stay away. We should avoid them..."

Herron nodded. Nath had told him all about the ISF, the General's hand-picked secret police. On Fiji, they were the thing that went bump in the night. They wore all black uniforms, targeted anyone the General deemed to be a threat and secured all of his most important facilities. By all reports, they were well trained and armed to the teeth.

Herron motioned for Nath to lead the way. Whatever else was inside, it didn't matter. The entire Fijian army could stand between him and this goal, nothing would stop him.

The General's roots in Fiji went deep, Herron had

reasoned, but the dictator was only able to hold onto his power because he was supported by American Oil and Gas. Unlike their Chinese rivals, however, the US company had no single facility on Fiji to destroy – no one way to physically dislodge them as Herron had with China National. Instead, the American corporation's vulnerability was in information.

Herron hoped that, somewhere, solid links could be found between the General and American Oil and Gas – and working in finance for the Ministry of Industry, Nath ought to know where to find all the dirt. So when he'd asked Nath about his job, and the Fijian had mentioned working on transaction records, Herron's eyes had lit up.

To the outside world, all transactions between the General and his corporate pals would be washed through shell corporations and foreign banks. If there was hard proof that American Oil and Gas was funding a tyrant, Herron could apply heat, melting the General's powerbase like a marshmallow under a blowtorch. But whatever financial details were stored on the computers in this building, the General obviously feared them leaking – the Ministry's network was contained entirely within the one place, air-gapped and totally inaccessible from the outside. No email, no cloud storage, no way to get to these secrets unless it was by on-the-spot physical interface with a machine.

If Herron wanted that data, he'd have to get it the hard way.

They crossed the street and entered the rendered-brick building through its front door. Inside, they found themselves in a stark white foyer that had nothing in it except a security desk with an armed guard seated behind it and barriers that required an identity card to pass through. It looked like any secure government building the world over.

Herron walked behind Nath as they approached the guard, hoping the desperate father would hold it together. While he'd promised to help, Herron had no way of knowing how Nath would react if they were exposed.

"You're here outside of hours, Jone." The guard looked up from his computer and stared at them. "Why?"

Nath leaned on the desk. "The General has asked for a meta-analysis of all known dissidents, including their families and friends. This man is going to help me."

"Okay." The guard's eyes shot to Herron and looked him up and down. "I haven't seen you around here before..."

Nath started to talk. "I—"

The guard held up a hand and cut Nath off. "I want *him* to tell me who he is, Jone, not you."

Herron locked eyes with the guard. "Why don't you pick up your phone, call the General and ask *him* who I am?"

The guard's eyes widened slightly and he stammered. "I... I'll need you to sign in before I can let you past."

Herron grunted and started to fill out the visitor log. He'd played on the fear that all dictators created in their underlings, where asking questions and getting yourself noticed could be bad for your health. He knew most low-level workers would take the path of least resistance, and since Herron had arrived with someone authorized to be inside, that seemed good enough for the guard.

When he was done, Herron waited while the guard tore the slip from the pad and put it inside a plastic badge holder. Herron took the ID and followed Nath through the security barriers. They exited the foyer and walked through the only door behind the security station, both smiling at how easy it had been to get past security and closer to their objective.

Then Herron's smile vanished.

"Not so fast, guys." A second guard was posted beyond the door. He held up a hand. "I'll need to run you through the metal detector, see what's in your pockets and frisk you."

Herron's eyes shot to Nath, but the look on the Fijian's face made it clear the extra layer of security was a new addition. Herron slowly walked through the metal detector. Nothing beeped, so he assumed the position and let himself be frisked. The guard did the job quickly and efficiently, finding nothing of note. Herron was glad he'd left his gun with Veena.

"Thank you, sir." The guard nodded at Herron and then turned his attention to Nath. "Step forward."

Nath looked nervous as he approached the scanner, although Herron wasn't sure why. They were unarmed and they'd made it through the hardest part – dealing with Herron's lack of identification. But here was Nath, visibly distressed, his eyes darting around the room and sweat on his brow.

The metal detector went crazy.

Herron had planned to take back the pistol that he'd given to Nath and Veena to keep them safe, but Nath had convinced him otherwise, saying Veena might still need it now they were in the endgame and the situation on the island was getting more dangerous than ever.

Clearly, he had taken it himself because now he was aiming it at the guard...

Herron sighed and approached the security man from behind, wrapped a forearm around his neck and press a hand over his mouth. His actions stopped the guard from screaming, but also compressed his carotid arteries, limiting blood flow to the guard's brain. He struggled, but Herron had him out in seconds.

As he eased the guard to the floor, he glared at Nath. "What the fuck were you thinking, bringing that thing in here?"

"I didn't expect this second checkpoint." Nath seemed unrepentant as he stared down at the guard and lowered the weapon. "There's someone in this building I wanted to take care of."

Herron held out his hand for Nath to hand over the pistol. They had a staring contest for a few moments, but whatever had driven Nath to bring the weapon into the dragon's den and compromise their mission, it was overridden by the threat in Herron's eyes. Nath handed over the pistol and Herron stuffed it in the waistband of his shorts.

"Who'd you want to *take care of*?"

"Inia Konrote." Nath lowered his eyes. "He's the head of the ISF. He sent the men to take Lynda. I hoped that if I took him hostage I could get them to free her."

Herron scoffed. "More than likely you'd have been killed trying. But even if you'd made it to your target, that's not how authoritarian regimes work."

"I have to try." Nath was unrepentant. "I'll do whatever it takes to get her out."

Herron stared at Nath, the other man's look as hard as granite. "I'll help you."

"Let's get the information you need first." Nath looked down at the guard. "Is he dead?"

Herron shook his head and then manhandled the unconscious man to a stairwell. Nath took Herron's lead, opening the door so Herron could drag the guard through it. When they were inside, Herron dumped the guard on the floor and used his handcuffs to restrain him to the handrail of the stairs.

Free of the heavy load, Herron opened the door back out to the lobby just a crack. Their little ruckus hadn't raised any alarms. There might still be time to do what needed to be done before the building's occupants knew what was happening.

Herron looked at Nath. "Let's keep moving."

* * *

"We're here." Nath stopped at a door and entered a code into its electronic keypad. "Follow me and don't touch anything."

He had led Herron through the building, up the stairs and to his office. They'd moved quickly, knowing the unconscious guard in the stairwell could wake up at any time and raise the alarm and that Herron didn't have the armaments for a protracted battle.

There wasn't much to Nath's office, just two desks crammed against opposite walls and barely enough room for two people to stand in between. There was the usual office-worker detritus spread across the desks, but nothing that suggested that the secret to bringing down the General was here.

Herron closed the door but stayed by it, listening for any sign of trouble, while Nath sat down and booted up his computer, ready to thrust himself deep into the information at the core of the General's regime.

An alarm started to wail through the building. Nath froze, his hands hovering over the keyboard. He looked at Herron, fear having replaced his earlier resolve. "The ISF knows we're here."

"Jacked up on their own self-importance? Dressed all in black? Armed to the teeth?" Herron's tone was dismissive, but he was well aware of how lightly armed he was to be dealing with full reinforcements. "I've dealt with their sort before."

"The ISF take you in the night and you never return," Nath said softly. "The rumor is that they bring you here to the basement. That's why I need to get to Inia Konrote. If I don't force him to release Lynda, we'll never see her again."

"Well, we better get on with it."

Nath resumed working. A moment later, the door handle started to turn. Herron gripped it, using all of his strength to hold it in place. After a few seconds, whoever was on the other side pounded on the door, shouting for them to open up. Herron kept his left hand in a locked on the handle and his right hand on the butt of his pistol as the hammering continued.

"I only need ten more seconds!" Nath was staring at a progress bar on the screen. "Okay, got it!"

Herron let go of the handle, letting the door open a little before driving it back with all his strength. As it slammed shut again, there was a cry of surprise, a sickening crack and a grunt of pain from the other side.

Whoever the door had hit probably had a broken nose now.

Herron drew his pistol, pulled the door open and stepped into the hallway. His surprise attack had downed one of the two men waiting for him, both security guards armed with batons and handcuffs. He aimed at the guard who was still standing and reached down to grab the wounded man's baton.

"You have a choice to make." Herron's voice raised over the noise of the alarm. He stood to his full height, the gun in one hand and the baton in the other. "I can shoot you or knock you out, but either way you're going down."

Herron knew which way it'd go. The guard was a middle-aged man with a wedding ring on his finger. He didn't resist as Herron lowered the gun, raised the baton and slammed him on the side of the head. The blow was hard enough to knock the man out cold, but not to fracture his skull.

With the immediate threat dealt with and the alarm still blaring in his ears, Herron stuck his head back inside the office. "Are we good to go?"

"Yep." Nath held out his hand, holding a USB drive. "I've got the information we need."

Herron led them out of the office, down the hallway and back into the stairwell. They descended to the third floor and then the second, planning to split up once they reached ground level. Nath would head out the front door and Herron would head on to the basement, where the ISF could be found.

They were halfway there when they heard footsteps coming up the stairs.

Herron stopped and looked at Nath. "Go. They don't

know you're working with me. Get the information out while I take care of the ISF and get Lynda back."

After a moment – and with barely another to spare – Nath nodded. He pocketed the USB drive, opened the door to level two and disappeared from sight.

Herron gripped his weapons and prepared for mayhem. He had to play for time to let Nath escape, then he could focus on finding Konrote.

Fighting in a stairwell was just fine by him, helping to reduce any numerical superiority his foes might have. Within a second, four Fijian men clad in black and armed with pistols came running up the stairs, clearly surprised to see Herron waiting for them.

"The ISF, I presume?" Herron aimed his pistol at them, pausing for just a second to see how they'd respond. "I don't want to kill you guys, I just want to talk to your boss..."

His foes raised their own weapons, making their choice.

He fired a double tap at the head of the lead man, whose brain exploded from the back of his skull and showered his comrades in gore, the sound of the shot deafening in the stairwell. It was an early point in Herron's column, but he was still heavily outnumbered.

The dead man dropped and rolled backwards down the stairs, his body getting in the way of the other ISF men who were trying to ascend. They instinctively looked down at the corpse, which let Herron drill the next man in line and then run back up the stairs the way he'd come.

He pulled the door open and exited the stairwell as shots pounded into the wall where he'd been only a split-second before. He ran down the hallway – there were office doors on both sides and he turned into one of them. It was empty, like the others, but it gave him one distinct advantage.

The ISF men came running after him, their heavy footfalls audible even over the piercing wail of the alarm. As they got closer, he aimed his pistol at the doorway, ready to fire if they burst in. Instead, as expected, they ran past. They had tunnel vision, chasing after him and not expecting he'd try to hide.

Herron stepped out into the corridor and fired two shots. Both men dropped without ever knowing their threat was behind them. He stepped closer, kicked their weapons away and then fired another shot into each of them to be sure he'd rendered the elite of the Fijian security apparatus completely inert. He still wasn't sure he'd get out of the building, but the chances...

"Drop your weapons!"

Herron turned to see four more black-clad operatives aiming weapons at him. "Hi guys."

One of the Fijians spoke, his voice filled with menace. "You're completely surrounded."

He was right. Another group had formed at the other end of the hallway.

Herron was trapped. He could either go out in a blaze of glory, or surrender.

He chose to live and fight another day. He didn't fear death, but surrender ensured the attention would remain on him, leaving Nath free to do what needed to be done with the information they'd secured.

It'd do nothing to help Lynda, though.

He knew the drill. He lowered his pistol to the ground, keeping his eyes on the ISF men. When it was on the ground, he put the baton next to the pistol, then dropped to his knees. He interlocked his fingers behind his head and crossed his ankles, remaining passive while the ISF men approached him.

When they had him totally surrounded, they kept him at gunpoint for almost a minute, until a new face arrived. He was different, a small bespectacled man in a business suit. He wasn't armed and he didn't seem particularly dangerous, but the ISF men were on edge around him. It could only be one man.

Herron raised an eyebrow. "Inia Konrote, I presume?"

"Correct." Konrote smirked. "Your little one-man insurrection is over."

Herron thought about the information on the USB, knowing the insurrection was just beginning. "In that case, I need to speak with you about Lynda Nath. You're holding her prison—"

"You haven't heard?" Konrote laughed, cutting him off. "I just ordered her release."

"Why?"

"My men caught Jone Nath on the second level and we made a deal. He's agreed to assist us in return for his family's freedom."

Herron didn't have time to process Nath's betrayal – a massive blow to the back of his head sent him reeling, falling face-first to the floor. Luckily for his teeth, the carpet cushioned most of the impact. He grunted as he took a boot to the stomach, knowing the ISF men were just getting started.

Somehow, it was less painful than the knife in his back.

9

HERRON GRUNTED as the baton hit him in the cheek, sending him sprawling to his hands and knees on the cold concrete floor. His jailer laughed and left the eight-by-four-foot cell, slamming the heavy steel door behind him.

After a second or two, Herron sat up on his knees. He spat out blood and then felt inside his mouth, checking no teeth had been dislodged. Everything seemed intact, so he shuffled over to the food the jailer had left behind. It was the same slop he'd eaten every meal for the past two weeks. It was awful, but it was sustenance.

The routine had been the same since his first day as a prisoner, when he'd overpowered a jailer and tried to escape. He'd exploited lapses in security, but failed to make it out of the prison. Captured again, he'd been beaten and starved for several days and then returned to his regular cell, where his VIP treatment had continued.

By now he'd become used to eating with blood oozing from his mouth. He took his time, because he had nothing else to do. Each day was twenty-three hours of darkness, followed by an hour for violence and feeding time. It was a strange kind of routine, but at least it gave him a sense of time. He spent that time thinking about how close he'd gone to ending Fiji's civil war before Nath's betrayal.

Like clockwork, after an hour had passed, the lights went out. Herron sighed, pushed the tin bowl into the corner of the cell and then retired to his bed – an inch-thick mattress on top of a steel base attached to the wall. He'd slept in worse places, so he simply closed his eyes and rested, preserving energy.

His revolution was over. Now, he was simply waiting for the axe to fall. It could be a week. It could be a day. Or it could be mere minutes. Whichever it was, he was proud that he'd chosen to make a stand instead of sailing away.

Now he was ready to die.

In the end, it was maybe only half an hour before they came for him, making him wonder why they'd bothered with the food today. It seemed like a waste. He opened his eyes as the lights turned on again, blazing like the sun. The cell door unlocked with a clunk and then screeched open.

He sat up on the bed as the jailer entered the room, followed a second later by another man.

Herron's eyes hardened. "Hello again, General."

The dictator looked a little worse for wear since the last time He'd seen him. He glared down at Herron like the westerner had killed his cat. "I told you to leave Fiji."

Herron said nothing. He didn't want to give the man he'd helped into power so many years ago and then failed to take down the pleasure of a response. The next words from the General's mouth would be confirmation of his upcoming execution, either by fiat or after a show trial.

Or so he thought.

The General sighed. "The information you stole from my network has gone public."

Herron barely kept the surprise off his face.

How had the USB got out?

After Nath's betrayal, he'd figured that his former ally must've handed the USB over to the ISF and explained the whole plan. Even if he'd held onto it for some sort of insurance to ensure Lynda's release, he must surely have been searched and interrogated, yet somehow...

The General's lips twisted into a snarl when Herron didn't respond. "What did you intend to happen once the financial dealings between myself and American Oil and Gas came out?"

"What did I *intend* to happen?" Herron rose to his feet. "I *intended* to put a bullet in your skull a decade ago, but through a fluke of timing and fortune you survived. But since I had to come back here, I *intended* to stay out of the troubles here. Instead, you had other ideas."

"I asked yo—"

"No," Herron said, cutting him off. "To borrow from Fox Mulder, the truth is out there, and now it's going to fuck with the control you've got here. Once it does, you bet your ass that I intend for you to eat that bullet."

The General shook his head. "I just wanted you to know, even though the files are public, you failed. American Oil and Gas will stay by my side. I have enough money, men and guns to withstand anything. The leak changes nothing."

"You clearly don't know how American corporate culture works," Herron scoffed. "I'm surprised it's taken this long for them to bail on you, honestly. I wouldn't be making any plans that don't involve your head on a pike."

The General clamped his mouth shut, turned and stormed out of the cell. The prison guard who'd taken a special pleasure in beating the snot out of Herron each day followed in his wake and slammed the door behind him.

Herron laughed, sat on the edge of the bed and waited until the lights went out again. Even then, he kept laughing. He'd lost faith in Nath and resigned himself to his fate, but somehow the government official had resisted revealing that he had the USB and finally released the information on it.

Herron hoped doing so hadn't compromised Nath or his family, but now they had a fighting chance. The FBI would be on American Oil and Gas like flies on shit. The Bureau didn't care for companies propping up corrupt foreign dictators, and the pipeline of dirty cash that flowed to the General would soon be blocked. Without it, the General couldn't pay his cronies, and as easily as that, his key supports would fall away. The General knew it, too. That's why he'd come to visit the cell.

Herron smiled. He felt like a man given another chance when he'd been certain he'd failed.

A man reborn.

* * *

The lights flared again and Herron opened his eyes. He blinked a few times and sat up in bed as the lock clunked and the door opened with an ear-piercing squeal. His regular jailer entered, baton in one hand and a meal tray in the other. Herron stretched and climbed to his feet, keeping his eyes on his captor.

"I won't be needing breakfast today," he said.

The guard laughed. The first time Herron had attempted to escape, he'd said the same thing. He'd taken the guard's baton, used it to knock him out and then fled the cell. He'd failed to escape, but that failure had revealed a key detail that he'd missed on the way in.

Herron waited for his moment to strike. First, the guard put the tray down on the ground, like he always did, before facing Herron and slapping the baton against his hand, like he always did. Then he smiled, cruel and sadistic, like he always did.

It was all as predictable as the Earth orbiting the sun.

What came next was a first, though.

Herron changed from passive prisoner to active attacker in an instant, stepping forward and grabbing the guard by the shirt. His jailer panicked, his usual position of superiority challenged, and tried to swing the baton. In the close confines of the cell, it was a mistake. Herron pushed him back into the wall and brought a knee up to his groin.

"Sadists like you shouldn't be able to reproduce." Herron spat on the man as he crumpled to the floor. "But if you stay down, you'll get the chance to do something useful with your life."

Herron watched for a second, but the guard made no move to stand, so he reached down, grabbing the guard's baton in one hand and the fork from his meal in the other. He pulled the door open and burst out of the cell, moving like a flash to the end of the cellblock, where he knew a guard station waited.

Herron pounded on the Perspex window of the guardhouse with his baton, then waved at the four guards inside. They stared at him with fury in their eyes, unable to believe he'd try to escape again after being foiled only days earlier.

None of them reached for a phone.

Herron felt a surge of satisfaction. He'd won the first battle. The guards were clearly confident enough to want to take him down alone, content to dispense another beating without calling for reinforcements.

He was happy to give them the chance. Taking a step back, he waited while they armed themselves and filed out of the guardhouse.

"You must have a death wish." The guard at the front of the group slapped his baton against his palm. Much older than his colleagues, he was a broad man, gnarled and weathered. "Stand down."

Herron gripped the baton tighter and kept his eyes moving between the guards, waiting for the first of them to make a move. He needed to time his strike perfectly. If he screwed it up, he'd suffer a fate worse than a beating – he'd be a prisoner again – and the unexpected release of the information by Nath would be wasted.

"Which of you is man enough to stick me back in a cell?" Herron grinned, taunting the men, hoping to provoke them into action. "Or do you need to call more help?"

The older guard laughed. "We've got all we need. You should've learnt your lesson the other day. All you scumbags do eventually. Some just take a few more beatings to get there."

"I'll give you one chance to surrender before I start breaking bones." Herron stepped back and the guards followed, moving away from their guardhouse. "I suggest you take it."

The leader said nothing.

Herron shrugged and seized the initiative, charging forward and slamming into the guards like an asteroid hitting a city. He started with the leader, a policy that'd never let him down, slamming the baton into his face. It was one of the top five blows Herron had ever delivered, a brutal shot that smashed bone and knocked the man out instantly.

As the leader dropped, the rest of the guards reacted like a shoal of fish, panicked in the presence of a great white shark. He continued on, swinging the baton like a crusader, full of righteous fury and purpose. He delivered more crushing blows and took a few shots himself, but they were nothing compared to the punishment he was dishing out.

He split the pack, leaving each guard with some wound or injury as he burst past them, then he sprinted for the guardhouse door. None of his foes reacted fast enough to stop his run to the endzone and within a moment he'd achieved his primary objective – he was alone inside the guardhouse. He slammed the door and locked it, trapping the guards in the common area in between the locked cells.

Within a second, it dawned on the guards what was happening. They pounded on the Perspex window with their batons, shouting desperate pleas and offers of a deal. Herron didn't want to hear it. Normally he wouldn't want to hurt men who were just doing their job, but the guards here had shown a predilection for savagery that Fiji could do without. On their watch, political prisoners were beaten, starved and kept in the dark. These were sadists, working for a sadist.

It was payback time.

He studied the control console, from which all access to and from this wing of the prison was controlled. Next, he looked around, hoping the Fijian authorities armed their prison guards as well as their cops. Sure enough, he spotted the exact same type of arms locker he'd found in the police station at Nadi.

He pressed down on the intercom button to speak to the guards in the common area. "What's the code for the arms locker?"

The guards looked at each other, then glanced as one down at their leader, who was still out cold and oozing blood onto the concrete. They weren't a group of men who were used to making decisions and they seemed to struggle with building a consensus. Their choice wasn't an easy one: arm their captor and possibly win some goodwill or otherwise face the unknown.

Herron quickly grew tired of the delay. "I'll make it easy on you. In 30 seconds, I'm going to open all the cell doors on the block, giving the prisoners free reign to kill the bastards who've tortured them for so long. That's you guys. But if you give me the code, I'll let you go into the cell I just escaped from and then lock it. You'll be safe when I release the hounds. Choose quickly. One. Two. Three. Fo—"

Finally, one of them blurted out the code. "Four. Seven. Two. Nine. Seven. One."

Herron lifted his finger from the intercom button,

walked to the locker and punched in the code. The digital panel lit green and the cabinet unlocked with a clunk. Herron smiled and quickly assessed the arsenal – shotguns, pistols, and riot gear. There wasn't quite as extensive a range as he'd found inside the police station, but it was good enough for his purposes.

He had the guns he needed, now he just needed to find an army willing to take up the arms.

He gestured with his chin at the guards, and they scampered to the cell he'd just been in. True to his word, he locked them in there with the press of a button, although he wasn't sure what they'd do for food until the dust settled. With a shrug, he started pressing all the *other* buttons on the console, each of which unlocked a cell.

At first, nothing happened, the prisoners no doubt thinking guards were about to open their cells and give them a meal or a beating. But after a while a few tried their luck, opening the doors to their cells and sticking their heads out.

Then the prison wing erupted with the fury of a long-dormant volcano, as men who'd been held in small spaces and treated inhumanely finally burst free.

Herron watched dispassionately as they emerged, shouting and whooping and laughing. Some started to trash their cells and the common area, some reunited with friends and family who'd been so close yet so far, while some simply took in the scene.

After the initial shock of their release, the mass of unshackled political prisoners approached the guardhouse and stared inside at the man who'd released them, waiting for answers. They clearly understood that freedom here, like anywhere else, came at a price.

He pressed down on the intercom button. "Which one of you is Alexander Pillay? Your wife told me you resisted the General. I need your help."

The pack – about twenty prisoners in total – hesitated, then glared inside the guardhouse as if it had only just dawned on them why he'd let them out. The dirty, scabbed faces of the prisoners flashed with hope, probably for the first time in months or years.

He was hoping that amongst these newly free inmates would be the Fijian Army Colonel who was married to the woman he had saved from the prison transport. The Colonel's wife had thought her husband might be dead, but Herron was betting he wasn't. The General liked his enemies to suffer. Herron, members of the Movement, their families... all had been imprisoned and assaulted, rather than killed outright.

It was a trend Herron hoped was universal. His revised plan would work without the Colonel, but the addition of the senior officer would help things along a heck of a lot.

Finally, a Fijian man who looked like he'd suffered more than the others stepped forward, until he was only inches from the Perspex. "I'm Pillay. Who're you?"

"I'm your ticket out of here." Herron paused. "I want to overthrow the General."

Pillay frowned, saying nothing as he assessed whether Herron was talking shit or offering a genuine chance to solve Fiji's problems. "I'm listening."

And as Herron explained his plan, Pillay's frown turned into a grin.

* * *

"Here they come!" Herron gripped his shotgun. "Don't let them take this position!"

He gripped his shotgun tight as a dozen men dressed in tactical gear flooded into the prison courtyard, at the other end of the row of cells from the guardhouse. They were sporting headsets and carbines, a step-up in class from the previous waves sent to recapture Herron, Pillay and the others.

Keeping low as the black-clad ISF men advanced, Herron popped up only to fire his shotgun and then duck before they could take him down. Although several of his allies had dropped around him, he knew they'd win. The ISF men might have better gear and weapons, but they were advancing in the open against a well-entrenched foe.

Herron and his motley crew were making them pay for every inch of concrete.

He pumped his shotgun then popped up to fire at another ISF man, who'd tried to find cover by opening one of the cell doors. It was locked. The man went down, his body armor failing to stop all of the 12-gauge buckshot, becoming one more body littering the hallway.

Herron fired the again, then tossed the empty shotgun behind him. He drew a pistol, ready to add to the mix of booming shotguns and chattering carbines, but by the time he got the weapon into a firing position the last of the ISF men had been taken care of and silence had once again descended on the prison.

They'd survived another wave.

Herron slumped down against the wall. He was

exhausted and almost out of ammo. The rest of his crew was no better. They'd fended off four attempts by the Fijian authorities to take back the guardhouse. First the prison guards had tried, then police officers, then the army, and lastly the ISF. They were tired, frightened and almost out of time.

"The General has lost patience." Pillay hunkered down next to Herron. "He's throwing his best men at us like cannon fodder."

"It's wasteful, but it's working." Only four prisoners were left to fight and they had barely a full load of ammo between them. "Your men better hurry."

"They will."

Herron closed his eyes, catching a moment of rest before the next wave. He had no way of knowing if his trust in Pillay was misplaced or not, but he had to rely on the man.

After agreeing to Herron's plan, the former Fijian Army colonel had made several phone calls. Before the lines had been cut by the authorities, he'd convinced several units of the Army still loyal to him to take to the streets, take control of Government House and to take the prison.

But if the troops Pillay had promised would come never arrived, all their efforts at holding the prison would be for nothing, no matter how hard they fought. Cut-off from the outside world, Herron and his fellow prisoners had no way of knowing whether the call for help was being answered. All they could do was hold out until they were relieved, or else make their death as costly as possible for the Fijian dictator.

Herron was comfortable with that. It had always been a risk when he'd uncorked this carnage.

He relaxed as calm descended for a few minutes, the defenders talking amongst themselves and doing their best to ignore the screams of wounded men. For Herron, it came easily. He'd never viewed a battlefield as a moral, ethical place. Combat was dirty and bloody and no-holds-barred, with only the victor earning the right to walk away alive.

His eyes shot open at the unmistakable boom of a tank's cannon, from somewhere outside. The battle inside the prison had expanded outside, but he had no way of knowing who was taking control out there: Pillay's men or the General's loyalists.

He was forced to file the question away for later, as one of the prisoners shouted a warning. Another incoming ISF wave. The remaining defenders climbed to their feet and took up defensive positions.

Herron's eyes widened; more men than ever were pouring in. "Conserve your ammo!" he shouted. "This is their biggest wave yet!"

He grunted as a computer monitor beside him was trashed by automatic fire, and ducked down just in time to avoid the raking bullets himself. His comrades weren't so lucky. Two more dropped in quick succession. Already the prisoners had felled at least a half-dozen ISF men, but the General's forces still were ahead in this most brutal of contests: he had more men to throw at them than they had bullets to fire back.

Herron popped back up and emptied his magazine, firing with sublime accuracy and dropping attacker after attacker. But his efforts were like using pebbles to stop the flow of a river. When his gun was dry, he searched on the floor next to him for another clip, but found none.

"I need ammo!" Herron's shout was barely audible over the roar of gunfire, more of it incoming than outgoing. "We're about to be overrun!"

"Not today, my friend." Pillay dug into his pocket for a pistol magazine. He tossed it at Herron, the grin on his face in complete contrast to their situation. "Have faith."

Herron caught the magazine, slammed it home and started to fire again as one of the other prisoners next to him dropped. "What makes you so confident? We're out of time!"

"There're only a few tanks in the Fijian Army," Pillay shouted. "And one of my most trusted friends is in charge of all of them."

"Well, he better move his ass, because we don't have enough ammo to fight off another attack."

When his last magazine was dry, Herron turned his attention to the arms locker. It was empty. They'd quickly burned through the stores and now he, Pillay and the one other surviving prisoner had nothing left. They ducked down behind the guard station, putting concrete between themselves and the ISF attackers.

Still the gunfire sounded, shot after shot after shot, and Herron began to think that even if the tank commanders were loyal Pillay, they'd still arrive too late.

Then he realized. All that gunfire he could hear... no rounds were hitting the guard station.

He peeked his head up out of cover for a second, hoping he didn't get it blown off.

"The cavalry has arrived."

Dozens of Fijian Army soldiers were pouring into the courtyard, gunning down the ISF men, who'd turned away from the guardhouse to fire at the reinforcements. When the last of the General's men had fallen, the soldiers advanced on the guardhouse with smiles on their faces. It made for a nice change. Herron stood up from cover and Pillay did the same, both unarmed and showing they were no threat.

One of the soldiers advanced ahead of the main group, stopped and saluted. "Reinforcements, as requested, sir. Good to see you, Colonel Pillay."

Herron looked to Pillay, then back at the soldier, then at *all* the soldiers. They were clearly devoted to this man, a potential rival to the General who'd been locked away but now had his chance to lead. And as the troops secured the guardhouse and tended to the wounded, Herron breathed a sigh of relief.

He'd come close to failing, but Suva Prison had been liberated.

The rest of Fiji was next.

10

———

HERRON FELT every bump and rumble as the old MII3 armored personnel carrier snaked through the streets of Suva. The ride was slow going, because the streets of Suva were ill-suited for the convoy of tanks and APCs heading for Government House, but they were making good enough time nonetheless.

"We're nearly there." Now dressed in camouflage gear, Pillay sat on the bench seat opposite Herron. "When I woke up this morning, I didn't expect I'd be taking over the country."

"When I woke up on a yacht a few days ago, I didn't expect to be helping you do it."

"We'll get you back to that boat soon, my friend." Pillay held out his hand. "Whichever way the final battle goes, Fiji owes you a great debt."

Herron took his hand and shook it. He'd swapped out his own prison clothing for some dragooned black ISF combat gear – only slightly bloodstained – and had also taken one of their carbines. It was a fine weapon and he'd scrounged plenty of spare ammo, so he was as well prepared as he could be.

After being relieved at the prison, Pillay's officers had explained the situation. Within minutes of the colonel's call for assistance, units loyal to their former commander had started communicating with each other, coordinating their plan to take control of the city.

It had taken an hour for the first troops to take to the streets.

Many of the General's former cronies had abandoned him quickly. Whether they'd sensed the balance shifting, anticipated the cash faucet from American Oil and Gas being turned off, or just grown sick of their leader, their reasons didn't matter. Only their actions did.

In Herron's experience, when power shifted inside a dictatorship it could often shift decisively, those who'd been ruled by an iron fist quick to free themselves once a little pressure is taken off. It hadn't surprised him to learn that within hours of the uprising many of the General's loyalist units had turned coat, either joining the campaign to unseat him or retreating to their barracks.

Those that were left had fallen back to Government House, where they'd dug in and prepared to make their last stand. Pillay's men had tried one frontal assault already, at the same time as they'd liberated the prison, but the attack had failed and casualties had been high. They'd decided to wait for their leader's arrival before trying again.

Pillay and his men rode in silence the rest of the way, receiving only the occasional status report from the convoy or other units posted around the city. Although there were still spot fires of conflict, the troops loyal to the General had mostly given up after their failure to extinguish the rebellion at the prison.

Now the battle for Fiji would be decided at Government House.

The APC ground to a halt. They'd arrived. Herron waited for the ramp at the back of the vehicle to lower, then let Pillay and the other soldiers out first, before picking up his carbine and following. At the bottom of the ramp, he stood and took in the scene.

It was breathtaking.

Rain was falling relentlessly, but despite that, fires were burning in a dozen places across Suva, belching smoke into the sky to meet the lightning that was occasionally brightening the dark clouds. While soldiers and vehicles had surrounded Government House in force, there wasn't a single civilian to be seen.

"The weather's certainly ominous." Herron ran a hand through his hair. "I'd hate to be the General staring out at the situation right now."

"Are you kidding?" Pillay scoffed. "He'll be hiding with Konrote while their remaining ISF goons and loyalist troops die to keep him safe."

He was about to reply, but held off as a man approached, wearing the uniform of a tank division officer and with gold and red crown rank insignia on his epaulettes. Herron didn't know the rank that represented, but the man carried himself with authority, so had to be somewhat senior.

"Major Reddy. It's good to see you again, my friend." Pillay briefly embraced him and then turned to Herron. "Major, this is my mysterious benefactor."

"Bob Sochi." The new arrival laughed. "We've heard

a lot about you. You took out the Movement's leadership, China National, and then American Oil and Gas."

"Something like that." Herron said, glad when neither man tried to pry more personal information out of him. They were smart. "I hope we can add the General to that list soon enough."

The tank commander shrugged. "We've taken control of the prison and most of the city, but the General still controls the rest of the island. He's dug in and there's enough loyalist forces inside the walls that dislodging him will prove difficult. Taking him down will be costly."

"I can take care of the General." Herron's voice was cold. "But first we need to discuss what comes after."

Pillay frowned. "What do you mean? I thought that I would—"

"No." Herron held up a hand. "It's not good enough to replace one military dictator with another. Things need to change. Fiji needs to change."

Pillay's eyes narrowed. "I don't like rules being added late in the game. What exactly did you have in mind?"

"There's a man from the Ministry of Industry – Jone Nath. He'll be in charge of the civilian administration of the island until the United Nations can arrange to have fair, internationally monitored elections. You two will be in charge of keeping the peace. Can I trust you both to keep your ambition in check and the army in line while that plays out?"

Pillay considered his words, then nodded. "We don't want to see another madman take over either."

Reddy chuckled. "Besides, we don't want you to

come back and do to us what you've done to the General."

"The only way that'll happen is if you screw up. But first we need to finish the job."

"What do you need from us?"

Herron grinned.

* * *

"Thanks guys. I'm good from here."

Two Fijian Army soldiers had escorted Herron to the rooftop, carrying his gear. They looked around, confirming there was nothing on top of the three-story building that'd harm Herron, then departed, leaving him with nothing but the tools of his trade for company.

That was fine by him. He'd prefer to do this alone.

He walked to the edge of the rooftop, to where the soldiers had dumped his gear – a rifle case and a man-portable missile launcher – and looked out over Suva, onto the back lawn of Government House. He'd been surprised the General had allowed this place to be built so close to the official seat of power, given the security risk it represented. Apparently it was owned by one of his cronies.

Besides, he probably never considered that approving the building could put him at risk.

Herron took his time preparing his arsenal. He assembled the rifle, loaded and sighted it, then examined the launcher. It was less familiar to him than the other weapon, but he was confident enough to use it if he needed to.

He was locked, loaded and ready to go.

Pillay had given him a headset. He put it on,

connecting himself to the command network of the loyalist units. "Guillotine is in place."

There was a short pause, then Pillay's voice came over the air. "Sledgehammer is ready to proceed on your call."

Herron was a man with a vast amount of experience in dealing death, but he'd never fired the starter's gun quite like this. He was looking forward to the show. "Execute."

Right on cue, the units surrounding Government House implemented their part of the plan, unloading tank rounds and machine gun fire at the compound. The fusillade unleashed a cacophony of noise, but Herron knew it'd do little more than that. The assault wasn't aimed at anything except the stone walls of the colonial-era fortress, which were as strong as steel.

But the effect on the defenders was instant.

Herron watched as they ducked down lower into their makeshift defensive positions – hastily dug trenches and sandbag emplacements – and prepared for the inevitable assault on the front gate. Inside, he expected it to be the same, the last of the General's true believers rallying for their do-or-die last stand.

He wondered about the psychology of such men in these kinds of circumstances, readying to sacrifice themselves to protect a tyrant against overwhelming odds. What drove them? Was it fear? Was it the hope of fantastic reward in the event of an unlikely victory? Was it simple delusion, a completely misplaced confidence in the face of oblivion?

He lifted his binoculars to his eyes. Whatever motivated those men, they'd probably live to reflect on it. Neither Pillay nor Reddy were confident of forcing the gate of Government House. They expected the loyalists to be heavily armed and ready to fight to the last, exposing their own troops to a massacre.

But it was the situation at the back of Government House that Herron was interested in. He figured the General had three options to respond to the attack on his headquarters. He could stay inside and wait until Pillay's men beat the door down, he could surrender before that happened or he could flee.

It took a while – and a few more tank rounds – but finally the General made his decision.

Herron watched through the binoculars as the General walked out the rear entrance, surrounded by Konrote and four black-clad ISF men. It seemed fitting the General would breathe his final breath as a coward, a man running away from danger while he sent the last of those who believed in him to their deaths.

The deposed leader and his entourage stopped near the back lawn of Government House and a moment later it became apparent what they were waiting for – a helicopter.

Herron heard the helicopter before he saw it. Flying in from behind him at high speed, it was a big military transport that'd have all the range it needed to get the General anywhere on the island. Pillay had told him that the General kept a loyalist air crew on standby at all times and that evacuation by helicopter was the plan in the event the General's position was threatened.

It was playing out exactly like that.

He placed the binoculars on the ground and picked up the boxy surface-to-air missile launcher, one of the few in Fiji's arsenal. He lifted it to his shoulder and looked through the sights. The chopper was lit up by the launcher's thermal imaging like a Christmas tree in Rockefeller Plaza, and instantly the weapon achieved a target lock.

Herron took a deep breath – a long, slow inhale and a relaxed exhale – and fired.

The missile closed the distance on the chopper within a second, like an asteroid blazing towards a planet. He felt for the pilot and crew, but Pillay had told him they were fanatics, the last Fijians ever to die under the General's reign of terror. No more people would be massacred, imprisoned, tortured or forced to live under the heel of a brutal dictator.

The helicopter exploded in a flash, brightening the night sky as its fuel tank blew. Flaming wreckage crashed down on the helipad, where the useless hunk of smoldering metal continued to burn like a star gone supernova.

Herron put down the launcher, its job done, and took up the sniper rifle, the second tool that'd help him prevent the General from escaping. As he aimed through the scope, the General seemed to be looking right at him, confused at the downing of his chopper and fearful of what it signified.

The Fijian dictator was a sadist who tortured his enemies, murdered their families, rewarded his cronies, sold out his country to foreigners. He had no redeeming features. He deserved to die.

Herron pulled the trigger.

The top of the General's head exploded, spraying brain matter over Konrote and the ISF men around him. The Fijian leader's body slumped to the beautifully tended lawns of Government House, an anti-climactic end of life for a piece of human trash. Herron then completed the job in short order, dropping Konrote right after the General.

He lowered the rifle and ducked down behind the concrete wall that lined the rooftop. He spoke into his headset. "The guillotine has dropped. The General and Konrote are dead."

Within seconds, Herron heard a confirmation from Pillay in his earpiece, followed by several subordinate commanders congratulating him on a job well done. Slowly, the fire from Pillay's forces slackened, then stopped entirely, as their officers told them it was over.

Within a minute, all gunfire had ceased.

Herron peered up again, using his binoculars to survey the scene. The ISF men had retreated inside Government House, leaving their leader's body crumpled in the grass. The defenders at the front gate were still hunkered down, unsure why the forces outside had stopped their attack.

Then came the first shouts over the loudspeakers, set up all around Government House by Pillay's men, informing the defenders their leader was dead and imploring them to surrender. The speakers also boomed a promise they wouldn't be harmed if they put down their weapons and put up their hands.

Herron watched as the defenders caucused in small groups, enlisted men and officers alike. A few took it upon themselves to run into Government House to check on the status of their leader, and it didn't take long before a pair of soldiers found the General dead on the lawn. It was over soon after.

Herron sat on the ground, his back against the concrete wall and the rain pouring down on him. He closed his eyes and let out a long sigh. It felt like he'd been fighting for months, when really he'd only been on Fiji for a few weeks.

When he'd killed the Master in London and destroyed the last remnants of the Enclave, he'd sworn he was done with killing. He'd sailed the Pacific and built a peaceful life. He'd been happy. Then the General had forced his hand and made him kill again.

He regretted the lives taken in the last few days, no matter the positive outcome. The only way he could live with it was if Pillay and Nath lived up to their end of the bargain and made Fiji a better place, and was comforted by the knowledge they were good men who cared about their country and its people.

He opened his eyes again.

The mission he'd started a decade ago was accomplished.

At last, he'd set things right.

He walked along the pier to his yacht, smiling when the vessel came into view. Although the Royal Suva Yacht Club's main building was still a burnt-out shell after the fire Herron had started, there were signs of life returning to normal on the island. Several boats had arrived or were preparing to depart, locals and visitors alike appeared happy, and the sun was shining brightly.

The same story was playing out across Fiji as the shackles of the General's control loosened. The troops were off the streets, all members of the ISF had been arrested and an inquiry had been established to determine if politicians and bureaucrats should also face charges. Life was returning to normal.

Herron had stuck around for a few days to keep an eye on the transition, but he had enough faith in Pillay and his men to do the right thing. He'd warned the Colonel that he'd be watching, no matter how much time passed and where in the world he ended up.

Now, it was time for him to go, but first there was one more thing to do.

He waited patiently by his yacht, looking down at his watch every few moments. Eventually, Jone Nath arrived, beaming with joy.

"Good to see you, Jone." Herron held his arms wide. "I'm sorry it took us a few days to figure things out."

Since escaping from prison, he hadn't been able to find out what had happened to Nath after his incarceration. As the dust of the revolution had settled and the military had established control, however, things had become clearer.

The two men hugged like long-lost brothers, men who'd spent less than a day together but whose lives had been connected by monumental events over the course of a decade.

After a second, Nath pulled away. "I'm sorry I betrayed you, my friend, but they had me cornered and they threatened to kill Lynda if I didn't tell them where you were."

"I can handle myself." Herron shrugged. Everything had worked out in the end, and it was hard to begrudge a man doing what needed to be done to save his daughter. "How did you get Lynda freed and still get the information out?"

Nath didn't respond immediately, suddenly self-conscious. "Well, I hid the USB somewhere they didn't want to search. Then I sent the data to *The New York Times*, the US Stock Exchange and the FBI."

Herron laughed. "You did well. We've taken down the General and his cronies, and now you and Colonel Pillay will forge a new path."

Nath's eyes widened. "Me...?"

"That's the price of your betrayal, my friend." Herron grinned. "I don't want the military taking over completely, so you're going to work with the Colonel to administer Fiji until elections can be organized."

Stunned, Nath placed a hand on Herron's arm. "I'll do my best. Fiji owes you a great debt. If you're ever in need of help, you simply need to ask."

Herron shook hands with him, one of the new leaders of Fiji. "Goodbye, my friend. I hope you and your family have a wonderful future. Give Veena and Lynda my best."

No further words were spoken, because none were needed. They'd been brothers in battle, now it was time to leave. Herron no longer wanted to be in Fiji, and Fiji no longer wanted him around to complicate things.

Herron reached down to his feet, where a small plastic bag was rustling softly in the gentle breeze. He grabbed the bag and handed it out to Nath. His Fijian friend took the bag with a questioning look, but Herron simply nodded. Inside was a fortune, enough to live like a king on Fiji for decades.

Without waiting for a response, Herron turned away from Nath, walked up the gangplank and onto his yacht. It felt like an eternity since he'd been aboard and he was excited to get back to open. As he set off, he waved once more to Nath, who'd waited on the dock.

The Fijian man waved back, both men knowing it was the last time they'd see each other.

* * *

Sometime later, safely back in international waters again, Herron set the yacht to autopilot and moved up to the deck. He stood at the back of the yacht, elbows resting on the railing, enjoying the serenity He'd fought so hard to get back to. Closing his eyes, he enjoyed the silence.

Until somewhere below deck, something banged, like a book being dropped on the floor.

Herron spun, drawing his pistol from the waistband of his shorts. Senses firing, he advanced, searching for a target as he walked down the stairs. If there was a threat, it was here between decks that he'd be most vulnerable, his body exposed to anyone who had nefarious intent.

He made it to the bottom...

...and saw Lynda standing in the corner of the cabin.

Herron lowered his pistol as she stopped picking up the contents of a shelf that she'd knocked off. She gave a bashful smile, but he kept his face stone-neutral, waiting for her to explain herself. He couldn't believe he'd have to return to Fiji after only just departing.

When she didn't speak he took a step closer to her, a stern look on his face. "What the hell do you think you're doing?"

Her eyes went down to the deck. "I told you I wanted to study postgraduate medicine in America or Europe. I want to see a little bit of the world first."

Herron scoffed. "And you decided to hitch a ride with me? You know nothing about me!"

"I know you saved me. I know you saved my dad. I know you helped to liberate Fiji. That's a good enough character reference for me."

"Then you're a fool, Lynda." Herron stuffed the pistol back into his waistband. "I'm taking you back home."

She crossed arms defiantly. "Fiji is my past. The world is my future."

Herron sized her up, suddenly feeling very old. In front of him was a smart young woman with the world at her feet. While he couldn't begrudge her for wanting more, taking the opportunity in front of her when she didn't have the resources to get it herself, he couldn't take her with him either.

He shook his head. "No."

As her face sank, her dreams crushed, Herron turned and headed for the wheelhouse. Although taking her back would cost him a few hours, he wouldn't have any trouble sailing back into Fiji after the solid he'd just done for the country. Lynda would return to her home and her parents and he'd be alone.

Lynda followed him, pleading her case, but he ignored her. When he reached the main deck, the sun was still shining and the sky was still a vibrant blue, but off into the distance something was different. A small Zodiac boat was approaching, with three or four figures inside.

He squinted into the distance. "Lynda, get back below and lock yourself in the bathroom."

She frowned at him, her protest cut-off mid-sentence, then tracked his gaze to the Zodiac. "Why?"

Herron hesitated, not sure he believed it himself.

"They're pirates..."

ABOUT THE AUTHOR

Steve P. Vincent is the USA Today Bestselling Author of the Jack Emery and Mitch Herron conspiracy thrillers.

Steve has a degree in political science, a thesis on global terrorism, a decade as a policy advisor and training from the FBI and Australian Army in his conspiracy kit bag.

When he's not writing, Steve enjoys whisky, sports and travel.

You can contact Steve at all the usual places:

stevepvincent.com
steve@stevepvincent.com

ACKNOWLEDGMENTS

Thanks as always to Vanessa, my family and friends, my beta readers - Gerard, Dave and Janice, Stuart Bache for the cover, Pete Kempshall for the edit.

Most of all, thanks to you, dear reader, for sticking with me for what is now my 10th book or joining somewhere along the line. It means the world to be able to do this.